The constellation of Sylvie

Also by Roderick Townley

The Great Good Thing
Into the Labyrinth
Sky

The constellation of Sylvie

A novel by
RODERICK TOWNLEY

A Richard Jackson Book
Atheneum Books for Young Readers
New York • London • Toronto • Sydney

Atheneum Books for Young Readers
An imprint of Simon & Schuster Children's Publishing Division
1230 Avenue of the Americas, New York, New York 10020
[(tortoise)(fish)(owl)]
The text for this book is set in Granjon.
Manufactured in the United States of America
First Edition
10 9 8 7 6 5 4 3 2 1
Library of Congress Cataloging-in-Publication Data
Townley, Rod.
The constellation of Sylvie: a novel / by Roderick Townley—1st ed.
p. cm.
"A Richard Jackson Book."
Sequel to: Into the labyrinth.
Summary: Twelve-year-old Princess Sylvie and the other
characters who live inside a storybook called "The Great
Good Thing" find that their book has been brought aboard
a spaceship on a doomed mission to Jupiter.
ISBN-13: 978-0-689-85713-3
ISBN-10: 0-689-85713-6
[1. Princesses—Fiction. 2. Books and reading—Fiction.
3. Characters in literature—Fiction. 4. Space flight—Fiction.]
I. Title.
PZ7.T64965Co 2005
[Fic]—dc22
2004014733

acknowledgments

I'd like to thank Capt. Alan Bean, the fourth person to walk on our moon, for his patience in answering my questions about space flight. Also helpful were Lisa Roberts, coordinator of the Educator Resource Center at Space Center Houston; Kevin J. Rosenquist, the ERC's former coordinator; Christopher Springob of Cornell University; and David F. Doody of the Jet Propulsion Laboratory in Pasadena, California.

The Governor's Arts Award and the Thorpe Menn Award provided much needed encouragement, and for those honors I thank the Kansas Arts Commission and the American Association of University Women. Thanks as well to Liz Brandt, Tim Brandt, and Trinity Brandt for their hospitality during my visit to NASA; Tim and Susan Norris for their bright spirits and helpful research; Joanne Baker for friendship and support; Russell Baker for many enjoyable discussions about space; and Wyatt and Grace Townley for inspiration throughout.

Ad Astra per Aspera
—Kansas state motto

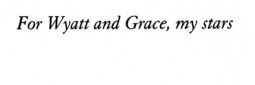

For Wyatt and Grace, my stars

contents

To the Reader

Sylvie wanted to write this preface, but I talked her out of it. It just didn't seem right for a fictional character—even a heroine like Sylvie—to step to the front of the book and talk to the Reader directly. Characters aren't even supposed to look *up* at the Reader, not that Sylvie paid much attention to that rule.

Anyway, she finally saw the point.

But we were all concerned about you. Yes, you, gentle skimmer, who is peering down onto this page. Now that Sylvie's story has stretched to three books (making it a trilogy!), we were worried that you might have trouble keeping everything straight in your mind. So we took a vote, and since I already wrote the preface to the previous book, I got the job.

Once upon a time there was a story called *The Great Good Thing*. It was a fine little book, filled with princes and villains and ogres and waterfalls, the works. But only a few copies were printed, and the last one happened to get burned up some years ago.

In the time of that terrible fire, Princess Sylvie managed to save the story by getting all the characters together and leading them into the mind of the book's last known Reader, a girl named Claire. There they lived in Claire's memory, showing up now and then in her dreams and exploring the wilderness of her subconscious.

But you know how you are. Admit it. Readers are forgetful. Before long, Claire no longer dreamed about the story. She dreamed about boys, and later about unpaid bills. By the time she got married and had a child of her own, she'd pretty much forgotten us. The characters suffered and some began dying off. After all, characters need Readers to feel fully alive, to have a reason to get up in the morning and act out their story.

It took our heroine Sylvie to save *The Great Good Thing* from vanishing altogether. It wasn't easy, but finally the story was all written down again and published. What a great day when the smell of new pages filled the kingdom!

Nobody could have foreseen the popularity of this new edition. The book was even uploaded onto the Internet. Readers became Viewers, and the characters had to learn a whole new way to act out their story. For one thing, they had to step *down* from line to line as the words scrolled upward. Let's just say there were accidents.

To make matters worse, a computer virus began infecting the plot. Whole pages disappeared and letters got switched around, creating dangerous wordpools. This all happens in the second book of the trilogy, *Into the Labyrinth*.

So does that clear things up? The first book led us through inner space (the Reader's subconscious). The second took us into cyberspace. And now? *Outer space.*

Fasten your seat belts.

Sylvie says hi.

—THE AUTHOR

The constellation of Sylvie

space

chapter one

Silence. The commas hung down, as if exhausted, below the lines of type. Even the exclamation points sagged. The king's oak trees stood deathly still, their leaves like leather gloves. In the entire forest of words, the only moving things were the tiny hands of a fly preening itself. Life was quiet these days inside the old book, now that the story had fallen out of fashion—in fact, out of print—but there had always been little scurrying sounds, the distant halloo of a shepherd, or the lapping of water on the shore of the Mere of Remind. This was different.

Just then the bushes swished loudly, and the head of a young girl popped up through the leaves. She was quite a sight. Her long brown hair was a tangle of coming-down braids, her travel cape covered with stickery twigs and smears of dirt. Her green eyes were all attention.

"What's happening? Can you tell?"

She was speaking to a boulder not far from where she

stood. Well, it looked like a boulder. In fact, it was a tortoise, its huge head swiveling toward her. Princess Sylvie often spoke to the animals in her story, using little endearments, and she seemed not to mind that they never answered. The tortoise was a particular favorite, and she sometimes sat on its back taking exceedingly slow rides around her father's kingdom. She'd never had time for such lolling about when the book was in bookstores—even on the Internet. She had begun thinking of that time as the good old days, forgetting how stressful it had been. Living inside a book can be more work than you'd think.

Not lately, though. What was the good of having an amazing story if no one read it? Yes, there was that one Reader, a lively girl named Angie, who for a while had carried the book around with her everywhere, sneaking glances at it at the dinner table or during important grown-up parties her parents gave at a place they kept calling the white house. (Did they have another house of a different color?) But now even Angie was gone.

Sylvie pulled several eucalyptus leaves from under her cape and fed them to the tortoise. "There you go. You like that?" The creature regarded her without expression, making a mess of the leaves in its beaklike mouth.

"That's all I've got!" Sylvie said brightly, then turned and ran over to an ancient oak tree that dominated this part of the forest. She scampered halfway up, quick as a squirrel, to her favorite perch. From there, the world looked the same as always, but it was as motionless as an illustration. Something had definitely changed.

Tucking her tongue against the back of her teeth, she let out a high whistle. The sound faded away immediately, as if the air were dead. She whistled again, louder than before. At last the sound of beating wings could be heard, and then a great snowy owl appeared over the rim of Humped Mountain and swerved toward her.

This was another magical creature, like the tortoise and the invisible fish that lived in the Mere of Remind; and like them, it was far larger than its counterpart in the outside world—large enough to pick up a gangly twelve-year-old and carry her wherever she wished. This always amazed Sylvie, because the owl was blind, its eyes milky and useless; yet it found its way. In the weary weeks between Readers she had tried to train the owl, although she was never able to tame it completely.

"Come, little one," she called, watching it sail closer. She often called her animals "little," no matter how enormous they were. "Take me to Laurel."

The bird's shadow blocked the sun, and Sylvie squinted up at the wings fanning above her. Sylvie had long ago sewn special eyelets into the shoulders of a harness she wore under her cape, so that the owl could lift her without hurting her or tearing her clothes. Now the creature slipped its talons through the loops and heaved itself upward, yanking the princess over the treetops.

The kingdom lay below them: the mountain and the Mere, shepherds' huts and pinewoods, and off to the west the dark walls of the castle. Usually farmers and trades-people would crowd the castle gates at this time of day, shouting and jostling. Sylvie veered nearer. The draw-bridge was deserted, and the lily-covered moat lay half in sunlight, half in blue shadow.

Blind though it was, the owl soared over the parapets, then turned south past the rock-strewn hideout of the thieves. Their leader, a rogue prince named Riggeloff, was sitting at a makeshift table outside his tent playing chess with Hroth and barely looked up as Sylvie sailed overhead.

The owl flew on.

"Here!" cried Sylvie, seeing a familiar figure standing on the cliff overlooking the Mere. "Let me down, please." Sylvie always felt a little burst of excitement when she saw Laurel. Over a century ago Laurel had written the original story; *The Great Good Thing*, she'd called it. It was a lovely book, but it didn't find an audience until years after her death. Then, through a kind of miracle, it had been republished with Laurel herself written in as a minor character. It was her form of heaven, she had told

Sylvie, to spend her afterlife inside her own story.

The bird plummeted to earth, landing so abruptly, it made Sylvie's stomach lurch. "We've got to work on that," she said a little shakily. The creature unhooked its talons and burst into the air.

The girl on the cliff was watching. "I was expecting you," Laurel said with a small smile. She seemed about Sylvie's age, but her face was narrower and her eyes, dark blue, had the look of someone much older.

"You were?" Sylvie said. "But I only just now decided to see you."

"Haven't you been listening to your Reader?" said the other. Her blue-hooded cloak matched her startling eyes. "I thought you always looked up at the Reader."

"I've been out in the forest with the tortoise."

"I don't mean in the last day or two."

Sylvie shrugged. "I guess I wasn't paying attention."

"Well, you've missed some interesting things. Pingree has stopped tormenting everyone with his jokes and sits scratching his thoughts between the lines of our story. Riggeloff has stopped his plundering and taken up chess. The thief Thomas has started bringing irises to Rosetta again."

"I knew about Thomas."

"But the main thing is . . . Have you *really* not been listening to the Reader?"

"You mean that girl Angie?"

"Of course Angie. She's the only Reader we've had for a year."

Sylvie waited.

"Well, she's been overheard talking about . . ." Laurel shook her head. "I know it sounds crazy, but she's been talking about a spaceship of some kind."

"A what?" Princess Sylvie, whose story is set in the Middle Ages, had never heard of such a thing. "A ship in space? But there's no water."

"Still."

"Where is the ship sailing?"

Laurel shrugged, but her eyes were alight. "To the stars, presumably."

"The stars!"

"You can't always go by what Readers say. Their dialogue isn't written down, and they don't remember what they said a minute ago."

"Are we supposed to be on it?"

"That's what I hear."

Sylvie was silent, her heart beating fast. "Laurel," she said, "remember how we used to talk about that?"

"Exploring the stars?"

Sylvie nodded quickly.

Her friend pressed her lips together. "It would be something, wouldn't it?"

Sylvie looked around at the unmoving grass and breezeless trees. "Is that why our story seems so . . . different these days?"

"Different?"

"I don't know. Stuffy. Airless."

"I think our book has been put inside some sort of container."

"Does that mean we've already begun sailing?"

"Oh, I think we'll know when we take off. These ships make more commotion than you can imagine."

Sylvie squinted at the distant castle. "Who's that down there?"

In the valley several horsemen trotted along beside an ornate carriage as it rattled over the drawbridge. The travelers headed east through a beautifully described countryside while a plume of dust rose behind them.

"Looks like the king's carriage," Laurel said.

"Oh, good!" said Sylvie, who was anxious to see her parents again.

But the next moment she forgot all about the king and queen as the ground began to shudder and shift beneath her. A powerful earthquake—that's what it felt like— began rumbling, shaking the squirrels out of the trees and knocking two of the king's guards off their horses.

The carriage veered into a ditch, a wheel spinning. Sylvie grabbed Laurel's hand to steady herself while the tremors grew more violent. Several boulders came loose and tumbled down the mountain, flattening two adjectives before coming to rest in the middle of the road.

"Laurel!" cried Sylvie.

Laurel's teeth were chattering from the vibration. She lost her balance and fell down, pulling Sylvie with her. A great weight seemed to be pressing on them, and Sylvie could not get back on her feet. As the seconds passed the heaviness increased, until finally she couldn't lift her head or keep her lips from parting, pulled aside by a force several times the weight of gravity. If the force grew any stronger, she thought distractedly, it might pull the flesh from her bones! She wanted to shout something to Laurel, but it was useless to try.

Am I dying? Sylvie wondered. She, who had never grown a day older in the decades since her book was first published—was she finally to find out what it was like to die?

chapter two

O h," she groaned, scarcely able to breathe. Soon the pressure began to let up, the shaking subsided into a steady vibration, and Sylvie found she was able to raise her head. She looked around. Her hand was still gripping Laurel's, and Laurel was holding on to the word *gnarled*, used to describe the tree root beside them.

"Are we sailing now?" Sylvie asked.

Her friend nodded nervously. "I think so."

"So it's really happening!"

A small brown rabbit poked a frightened nose out from behind a rock. Sylvie watched it hop onto the rock and sniff about, its ears twitching. Then, as Sylvie watched, the rabbit stepped into space.

"Laurel?" Sylvie's voice had a quaver in it.

"What is it?"

Princess Sylvie nodded at the rabbit, which was floating in the air.

"Oh!" said Laurel, standing up. "How strange!" She

wobbled and almost lost her balance. "I feel light-headed," she said with a giggle.

"You're light-*footed*," Sylvie returned.

Laurel looked down and saw that her feet were several inches above the ground.

Sylvie got to her feet and immediately floated off, gradually slowing until she hovered like a balloon above her friend. "Hey! How do I get down?"

A sheep drifted by, a few feet below her.

"I don't know!" cried Laurel. "We seem to be weightless, or nearly. That happens in space."

"We're not in space," Sylvie called down. "We're in a book!"

"But the *book* is in space!"

"Do you think the owl could help?"

"Try."

The princess gave a piercing and very un-princesslike whistle, then looked out over the water. After her second whistle she saw a dark spot wavering toward her. It was the owl, having a hard time in reduced gravity. The downswing of its wings caused it to veer upward, and each upswing caused it to sink. Still it struggled, eventually circling the princess.

"Help me down, please, dear bird," called Sylvie.

After several attempts it managed to snatch one of Sylvie's shoulder loops and pull her roughly to the ground. Sylvie quickly filled her pockets with stones, relieved to discover that a small amount of gravity remained.

"Help!" a man's voice called from over the hill.

"That sounds like Godric," said Sylvie. She filled her pockets with largish stones and carefully stood up. "I see him. He's stuck in a tree. Let's bring him some stones."

"Maybe we can tie a stone around the owl," Laurel suggested. "It might be easier for him to fly."

"Help!" Prince Godric cried again.

Sylvie struggled to him and helped him climb down. His lip was bleeding, but she didn't ask how he'd hurt himself. He was often hurting himself these days. According to the story, Godric was under a spell that kept turning him into a horrible humpbacked creature known as the Keeper of the Cave. He fought against this other self, which often meant punching himself in the nose, or trying to wring his own neck. It wasn't pleasant to watch.

But now he was just Godric again, with his feet on the ground and stones in his pocket, grateful for Sylvie's help.

Suddenly everyone, even the owl, was pinned to the ground as the vibration resumed. Sylvie felt a great heaviness pressing her chest. It wasn't as intense as the first time and didn't last as long, ending abruptly in a way that flung her off the ground and into the branches of a sycamore.

"Ouch! What was that?"

A rabbit whizzed over their heads out of sight, as if flung by a catapult. "I'm not sure," Laurel called to her. "From what Mr. Fangl has told me about such things, it could be the 'second stage.'"

Sylvie didn't answer at first. She was looking at her arms, which were floating straight out in front of her, as if she were a sleepwalker. "Why are my arms doing this?"

"Not enough gravity to pull them down," Laurel said. "Pretty soon there'll be hardly any at all."

"Fangl!" called out King Walther, poking his head out the window of the overturned carriage. His voice sounded desperate. "Bring me Fangl!"

The king's guards, one of them tangled in a gore bush, the other hovering beneath his floating horse, were in no position to help. It took Sylvie, with the aid of the blind owl, to fetch Norbert Fangl from his study in the castle. Fangl was Sylvie's geometry tutor, the only character in the book with any scientific background. He was also, like Laurel, based on an actual person, so he knew about the outside world.

Over the next hour, at his direction, ropes were strung at waist height from the carriage to the castle. Fortunately, there was plenty of rope in the castle's storerooms, but they'd need even more if this weightlessness kept up.

Young Godric gripped the guide rope tightly, his eyes darting about fearfully. One at a time, the royal family, as well as the Chief Councillor and the queen's lapdog Lulu, were helped out of the carriage. The councillor's toupee immediately floated off his head and out of reach. Aside from that, things went fairly well until several characters forgot to hold on to the ropes. Queen Emmeline, who could be seriously upset at the sight of a cracked teacup, nearly *fainted* the first time she found herself turning slow somersaults in midair. Lulu, several feet below her, squirmed and whimpered. Somehow King Walther managed to maintain his dignity, but it wasn't easy: He was suspended upside down twelve feet above the moat.

Time passed interminably.

"A good thing we don't have Readers," the king grumbled when he was back in the great hall of the castle and tied on to his throne with velvet ribbons. He felt safer inside with a ceiling overhead.

"This is as bad as that, as that . . ." Queen Emmeline waved her hand helplessly in the air.

"Do you mean the Internet, Mother?" said Sylvie.

"That's the word. Nothing weighed very much, as I remember, and the food tasted terrible."

"Yes," Sylvie said. "*Virtual* food." She made a wry face.

"But at least you didn't float about like a . . ." Again the helpless gesture. "Like a whatnot!"

"If our latest Reader is correct," said King Walther, nibbling on the end of his mustache, "we may be traveling to the stars. What are you *cackling* at, Pingree?"

The court jester, a small, twiglike creature with a comically mournful face, was snorting behind his cap. He clapped the hat on his head and tilted his skinny body to the side as if to get a better look at his master. "But there *are* no stars, Sire," he said. "Look around you. On the darkest nights do you see stars?"

"Because we don't see them does not mean they don't exist."

"But that's precisely what it means!" In his excitement Pingree had let go of the guide rope and begun rising off the page. Sylvie grabbed his sleeve and pulled him back. "A moon, yes," he went on. "During the night scenes in our book there is always a bright full moon, but nothing star-shaped at all. I would have seen it."

"Several of us," the Chief Councillor broke in, frowning, "distinctly heard the Reader speaking about stars."

"The Reader is an ignorant girl!"

"She knows more than an ignorant jester!"

"I'm not so ignorant as you think," Pingree snapped back. "I have ears."

"Indeed," the councillor growled. "Little pointy ones."

"Are you saying," said King Walther slowly, "that you know something we don't?"

Pingree looked sly.

"Good heavens!" the king burst out. "If you know something, tell us!"

The jester flinched. He knew not to push too far. "Well, Sire," he said, taking off his green cap and twisting it in his hands, "being a fool and not having important affairs of state to attend to . . ."

The king gave an impatient flick of his hand.

"I've been able to observe the Reader at odd moments. I learned, for instance, that she's the daughter of a president."

"A what?"

"It's like a king, minus the ermine."

"Oh, yes, of course," said Walther vaguely.

"Anyway . . ." The jester paused, gazing upward like a professor lost in thought.

"Go on!" said the king, coloring.

"Doesn't it amaze you, Sire," said the little man, rising on the toes of his pointy green slippers and lowering himself, "the way Readers will discuss the most personal, private things while a book is lying wide open in front of them, as if we couldn't hear what they say?"

"I never thought about it. In fact, I'm not thinking about it now."

"I mean, we're fictional, not stupid."

"Are you planning to tell us what you know or not?"

"Yes, yes, of course." He began rising again onto his toes.

"Stand still!"

"What I meant was, I heard her talking with her father about some sort of space capsule. I couldn't see very well because she had the book mostly closed, with just her finger holding her place. Don't you hate it when Readers do that?"

"Do what, for heaven's sake?"

"Intrude their fat fingers into our kingdom."

"Pingree, get to the point!"

"Yes, Sire. Well, he was showing her some of the things going into the capsule. There was a metal plaque with greetings in various languages from the people of planet Earth. Also something called a baseball, a small flag, some small flat discs . . . Yes, and a book."

"A book, you say?"

"At first I misheard and thought it was written by Rosetta Stein, who is a character in our own book."

"We all know Miss Stein."

"But then the president said the name again, and I realized the first name was Ein."

"What kind of name is that?"

"I don't know, but whoever this Ein Stein is, he must

be quite a storyteller. His book was the only one they were putting in the capsule."

The king was getting restless. He could take only so much information. "What does this have to do with us?"

"A great deal, because that was when Angie got her brainstorm. I could see her finger twitch inside our book, where she was holding her place. Actually, I could feel it, because she was tickling the back of my leg."

"Would you get *on* with it?"

"Well, when her father went over to the window for a minute, his twitchy-fingered daughter slipped the dust jackets off the two books and switched them!"

"She what?"

"She slid the Stein book into her pocket and laid our book by the container."

"Are you sure?"

"Sure as I am of anything. A girl's impulsive act, and just because she thought *The Great Good Thing* was a better story than that other one."

The room was silent.

"So you're saying . . . ," the Chief Councillor began.

"That we're here under false pretenses?" Pingree supplied. "Here, where we aren't wanted? Doesn't do much for the ego, does it?"

"You've got ego enough for all of us," retorted the councillor, reaching up to check on his toupee. He'd had it glued back on, but it wasn't right.

"Please!" the king said. "I'm trying to think!"

Whatever thoughts the king was developing in his noble but slow-moving mind never reached the point of expression, because at that moment, without warning, the top of the castle lifted away, sending a delirious gust of air through the throne room. A breeze, at last! It lifted Sylvie's hair and blew a proclamation off the king's writing table. At once an enormous face appeared—a Reader no one had ever seen before—peering down into the storybook kingdom.

"Omigod!" the new Reader cried out. "Look at this! Matt! Wink! Come here. *This isn't Einstein!*"

chapter three

The king stared upward, his mouth open. The Reader, a pretty young woman with alert eyes, stared frankly back.

"Matt!" she called to someone out of sight. "You've got to see this."

A man's face appeared beside the young woman's. It was a settled, lived-in face, pleasant in its way, though hardly handsome. Dependable-looking, Sylvie thought. "You've broken the seal!"

"I know, but there's hardly anything to read around here."

"Kara," he said with a frown in his voice, "we were ordered to keep this capsule airtight."

"Sorry. But wasn't this supposed to be Einstein's *Special Theory of Relativity?*"

"Of course."

"I thought I'd read it again, for fun. But look!"

The man's face came closer, his eyes scanning the opening lines.

Sylvie nudged her father, who was still staring. "Oh!" said King Walther. "Right-ho." He stood up beside his throne, holding on to the guide rope to keep his feet on the ground, cleared his throat, and began the familiar opening scene of their story.

"Father," declared Princess Sylvie, projecting her voice upward, "I cannot marry Prince Riggeloff."

"Not marry Riggeloff?" The king gave a sideways glance at the two Readers above him. "For heaven's sake, child, he is handsome, rich—"

"Kind, brave," Princess Sylvie interrupted. "Yes, I am aware of his qualities."

"He has everything."

Sylvie edged around a half-page illustration. "So have I," she replied.

"You don't have a husband!"

Suddenly the book closed, and then immediately opened. Then it turned onto its side as the Reader named Matt pulled off the dust jacket and read the title on the spine: "*The Great Good Thing*, it says. It's just a silly kids' book."

He snapped the book shut, throwing the king's court into darkness.

"Ow!" cried Sylvie, banging her head against a suit of armor. After a moment the backup lights came on. Queen Emmeline, still tethered to her throne, was flustered but unharmed; the ladies-in-waiting had tumbled over one another, their legs sticking out from their petticoats in all directions.

Pingree was badly upset. He'd rolled across the floor and halfway up the wall, where he remained, helplessly suspended. *"Silly kids' book?"* he hissed. "We'll see who's silly. Get me down, somebody!"

"We have Readers again," murmured Sylvie with a smile.

Sylvie's friend Laurel emerged from the confusion of legs. "I think they're called astronauts," she said.

"Whoever they are," humphed the queen, "they should learn manners! And that girl! Did you see her hair? Someone should lend her a looking glass!"

"I think," said Sylvie, "they call it a ponytail."

"I can believe it." The queen turned an eye to Laurel, who had once been an actual person and knew about life outside the book. "What do *you* think?"

Laurel curtsied deeply. "It wouldn't be my choice, Your Majesty."

"I hope not."

"But other than that," said Laurel, "how are we liking our first trip into space?"

"Terrible!"

"So far," added the king, "we have enjoyed all the disadvantages and suffered none of the advantages."

"Oh, I don't know about that," a voice sang out from somewhere outside the hall.

Sylvie whirled around to see a tall young shepherdess, arms outstretched, sail in through one of the great arched windows. The woman circled the thrones three times and slowly came down, landing on her big toe.

"Rosetta!" cried Sylvie. "How did you *do* that?"

Rosetta Stein laughed, her long chestnut hair unfurling behind her like a playful animal. "Gliding around is the easy part," she said. "Coming down takes practice."

"Miss Stein," said the king, "do you think the rest of us could learn to glide?"

"Why not?"

"But how do you get *down*?" cried Pingree, who had been attempting, without success, to climb down the wall.

"Centering," declared Rosetta Stein, who before she was written into the book had been a yoga teacher.

"Centering?" Pingree made a sour face.

"It's in the yoga training. You close your eyes and center yourself, breathing deeply, and *feel* yourself grow heavier. Before you know it, you're back on the ground."

"Feel," he spat. "I *feel* myself growing angry!"

"Those feelings won't get your feet on the ground."

"Just get me a ladder."

"And if the ladder floats away?"

As if to underscore her point, a flagon of ale rose from an oaken side table. The vessel tipped and the ale spilled out, but it didn't splash to the ground. It merely spread through the air like a giant amoeba.

"Are you saying," said Sylvie slowly, "that we could act out our story for Readers by *gliding* our way through it?"

"Hadn't thought about that," Rosetta said.

"I don't see that we have a choice," Laurel put in. "Otherwise, we'd be hanging on to ropes the whole time."

"This might be fun." The corners of Sylvie's mouth kindled into a smile. "We could skip over some of the descriptions we usually get tangled up in."

"Readers skip over them already," snipped Pingree. "Is somebody going to get me down?"

Sylvie stretched her arms out tentatively and gave a little upward push with her toes. She began to rise.

"Good, Sylvie!" said Rosetta. "Now just twist your body to the side."

Sylvie did as she was told. "It's like swimming!" she said, marveling.

"Well, not quite. You have to push off from something every few seconds."

"Yes, I see." Sylvie coasted up to Pingree, who was holding tightly to the wall. "Try it," she said. "Let go."

Pingree looked doubtful.

"Oh, come on, take my hand. I'll help you down."

The jester closed his eyes tight and let her grasp his bony fingers.

"Remember your centering exercises," Rosetta called up to her. "Find your gravitational center. Think of a thread reaching from you to the center of the page. Feel it anchoring you."

Anchor, anchor, thought Sylvie. She began sinking, pulling the jester with her.

"That's it," said Rosetta. "Reel in the line. Reel it in."

Sylvie's feet lightly touched the flagstone floor. Pingree opened his eyes as the courtiers burst into applause. He so seldom had the chance to hold Princess Sylvie's hand that he didn't want to let go of it.

"Me next!" cried Laurel.

Rosetta gave gliding lessons to each person in the room, even, finally, to the queen, who had been reluctant at first. The only person to refuse absolutely was Pingree, who was holding to a column. He was skeptical of the whole business, even when he saw his monarch, King Walther, floating overhead.

"What are you afraid of, Pingree?" Sylvie called from the top corner of the high-ceilinged chamber.

"Looking foolish, for one thing," Pingree retorted. "Breaking my brains, for another."

"Interesting," said Laurel, who was practicing somersaults over the chandelier, "a fool who's afraid to look foolish."

"Come, Master Pingree," coaxed the king. "I need you here beside me."

"I prefer not, Sire."

"Well, I won't command you." The king swung through the air from one end of the throne room to the other, chortling as he went.

All the tumbling and swooping and falling gave the royal court the air of a drunken party. Never had there been so much laughter or so many whoops of surprise. When the hilarity was at its height, the king's parrot lifted its orange head, then shifted from one leg to the other and squawked, "Reader! Reader! *Rawwwk!*"

All at once the vaulted ceiling lifted away, revealing the face of the ponytailed woman named Kara.

"Quick! To your places!" called out the king; but he couldn't even get to his own. His concentration was off, and he wasn't able to descend. As a result, his first few lines were delivered while he hovered over the heads of the courtiers.

"What a strange book." The Reader shook her head.

"What?" It was the voice of the astronaut called Matt.

"Seems to be a family of circus acrobats. Now, let me read."

For the next three chapters Sylvie didn't have a moment to look up at this interesting new Reader. After the villainous Prince Riggeloff had sent his thugs to steal the royal treasure, the action moved outside the castle, into the forest, atop Humped Mountain, and beneath the treacherous waters of the Mere of Remind. Sylvie and the others had to deliver their lines and get from one scene to the next without the benefit of gravity.

"What a *very* strange book," said Kara again. She was reading the chapter where Riggeloff's ruffians chase Sylvie through the forest. Finding herself at the edge of a cliff, Sylvie spurs her donkey to leap into space, landing in the Mere far below. Attempting the scene while weightless was a disaster. Sylvie and her little donkey remained suspended above the water for the longest time, until the princess managed to "anchor" her mind. She lowered herself and her donkey so slowly, they didn't even make a splash. Riggeloff's men, meanwhile, shot volleys of arrows after her; but the arrows sailed about aimlessly, eventually coming to rest in midair, as if on invisible shelves.

"I *like* this strange book," said Kara.

"What are you reading?" It was a male voice, different from the other, sharper sounding.

"Take a look."

The kingdom trembled as the book was passed to the new Reader. An impatient face frowned over the Mere of Remind. Sylvie, treading water, looked up at jaggedly handsome features and darting eyes. His forehead was narrow, giving him the drawn-together look of someone who was constantly working math problems. Naturally, entering the story in the middle, he could make no sense of it.

"Looks like gibberish to me."

"It's a *story*. A pretty good one."

"I don't like stories."

"Wink, I'm sure that isn't true."

"To me? The most beautiful story? An equation."

She laughed musically, three notes, like a bird. "It's hard to curl up with an equation!"

"Believe me, Einstein's the greatest storyteller who ever lived."

"Are you *trying* to be weird?"

"You've got four years to find out. Two to get there and two back."

"Don't remind me."

"We're lucky," the astronaut called Wink continued. "It took *Galileo* six years to reach Jupiter, and that was unmanned. They've speeded things up by four whole years."

"Dinner!" called another voice, belonging to the man named Matt.

"Oh, boy," said Kara, laying the book faceup. The pages pointed straight out like the quills of a nervous porcupine. "Four years of space food!"

"*Floating* space food," said Wink. "We can always cook up your lab mice," he said. "For variety."

"You leave my little guys alone. We'll be experimenting with their great-great-grandchildren on the way home."

Matt gave a little "Hmm."

"What?" Wink's voice.

"Nothing. I was wondering how long before we know everybody's jokes."

"About ten minutes. Of course, you don't have any."

"A good thing we like one another," Kara put in.

"Yeah," said Wink. "Imagine if we didn't?"

The conversation dwindled as the crew finished eating and cleared away the trays.

Sylvie and her father looked at each other.

"Four years?" the king murmured.

She lifted her shoulders in a shrug. Even that small gesture took her an inch off the page.

The king gnawed his lower lip. Usually he just nibbled his mustache. "A few *days* might be enjoyable. Floating is certainly a remarkable thing."

Sylvie decided not to mention her own thought, which struck her just now with force: If their book was left in some container on an empty planet in the farther ends of space, they might be bobbing around like this forever!

"How do you suppose," said Matt, "that funny little book ended up in the capsule?"

"Somebody's idea of a joke," said Wink.

"It's like something a kid would do," said Kara.

"Not a lot of kids in the NASA program," said Matt, "except for you, Wink."

There was a burst of static. "*Heartland*, this is Mission Control. Over."

"Roger, Houston, this is *Heartland*," said Matt.

"We have two things for you. One, we need you to

start your sessions with the Performance and Affect Monitor."

"But we've only been up here a week."

"PAM needs initial data now, so we can compare it later. Also, we've got a couple of flight plan updates, when you're ready to copy."

"Standing by for your updates. Over."

"Okay. If you'll look on page 70-B of your CSM checklist . . ."

At some point in the next twenty minutes of instructions, someone gently closed *The Great Good Thing* and slipped a rubber band around it.

PART TWO
fate

chapter four

The elastic band stayed around the book a long time. With no calendars in the kingdom, it was impossible to tell how long. Many sundials, certainly.

Life between the pages returned to normal, except that instead of strolling from the castle to the Mere, or from the courtyard to the Privy Council, you'd glide there. You could walk, of course—by now the kingdom was cobwebbed with guide ropes. Some of the older courtiers depended on the ropes, but mostly it was the peasants, peddlers, and servants who used them. Shepherds, too. Their flocks, floating on ahead, were fitted with leashes that the shepherds held in one hand while their free hand held to the guides.

The forest animals had the hardest time in microgravity; and at Princess Sylvie's urging, the king set up an Animal Rescue Council. Each morning servants would be sent out to help confused squirrels, rabbits, and an occasional deer from their perches in midair. It became part of Sylvie's routine too. At dawn she'd check on the animals she especially loved: the great tortoise, the blind owl, and the mysterious invisible fish. She often found them in distressing situations. As often as not, the huge fish, clear as a glass house, would float out of the Mere and flop about, gasping, several feet above the water. It took all the king's horses and a dozen ropes to get him down again. It was easier if the fish had been there all night, because then he'd be dried out and curling at both ends like a piece of parchment. At such times Sylvie could get him down by herself. She'd dunk him back in the water and watch as he expanded to full size, his gills twitching with gratitude.

Of course, the humans were the prime concern; and almost the first thing the king did was order everyone, starting with officials of the court, to take gliding lessons from Rosetta.

Prince Riggeloff didn't care for the idea of taking lessons, or even suggestions, from a woman, but he knew that if he was going to commit robbery and mayhem, as the plot required, he needed to be able to get around—and when pursued, to get away. Still, there was a glower in his glance when he and his men showed up for lessons. Because they were so disruptive, Rosetta taught them separately from the others.

"What's our torture today, wench?"

She flashed him a look. "Landings. That's what you have the most trouble with."

He made a sound in his throat that she recognized as disgust. Still, he took the lesson and did his best, although he had no idea what she meant by "Access your inner gravity." Still less did he understand "Drop down into your belly."

"What in blazes!" cried Hroth, the heftiest of the prince's ruffians. He continued drifting toward the roof of the great hall, despite furious efforts to come down.

"Do as she says or I'll knock your teeth in!" growled Riggeloff, who was bumping his head against a rafter.

The only member of Riggeloff's crew to make real progress was Thomas. The youngest of the thieves, with unmanageable dark hair and surprised-looking eyes, he would have done anything for Rosetta. As a villain, he was a washout. So simple a thing as stealing a pear from a peddler would throw him into tumults of guilt. The truth is, he was made for love, not lawlessness, and he thought Rosetta the most beautiful creature he'd ever seen.

"Close your eyes and feel yourself magnetized to the page," Rosetta intoned.

Lids lightly closed, Thomas drifted lower till the toe of his shoe brushed the floor.

"Bravo, Thomas!" cried Rosetta, clapping her hands.

Riggeloff, hanging on to a rafter, scowled down. "How does he *do* that?"

"I can do it too!" cried a young man sailing in through the arched window. It was Godric, his head bandaged and his cheek bruised. But he was smiling as he grasped the top of a column and gave himself a spin, twirling downward. He bowed as Rosetta and Sylvie applauded.

"That's not so hard," Thomas retorted. He ran across the room and threw himself into a forward roll that somersaulted him right out the window.

"Leaving so soon?" Prince Godric immediately closed

the window and latched it, then threw Rosetta a satis-
fied look.

"That wasn't nice," Rosetta said.

"I suppose not, but he was showing off horribly."

"And what were *you* doing?"

"Both of you," piped up Pingree from behind a pillar,
"are love-struck lunks."

"The fool is right," said Riggeloff, making his way,
hand over hand, down the rough stone wall.

"You're jealous," said Godric, eyeing the prince,
"because you're incapable of love."

"At least I have my feet on the ground."

"Actually," Rosetta said, smiling, "you don't."

Pingree gave a chuckle but cut it off when Riggeloff
glared.

Reaching the floor, Riggeloff flung his cloak over his
shoulder and strode away. That was his intention.
Actually, he walked several feet into the air, his legs
punching through space as if pedaling an invisible
bicycle. "Somebody get me down from here!"

Sylvie felt for him. Riggeloff's intelligence was consid-
erable, but his character wasn't written in a way that
allowed for humor. "Here," she said, "let me help."

"Pah!" But in the end he let her guide him. He nodded curtly and, holding to the ropes, lurched toward the
door, where he collided with Thomas, who was running
in from outside. Thomas, a much lighter man than
Riggeloff, staggered backward.

"What do you think you're doing?" the prince
snapped.

Thomas stared blankly for a few seconds, catching his breath. "I was just," he said, "coming back to kick some sense into that man over there."

Riggeloff's eyebrows lifted. The idea of Thomas actually doing something violent was surprising. "Well," he said, "don't let me stop you."

Thomas stepped into the center of the hall. Godric looked down at him from the chandelier, where he was now swinging. For a man in conflict with his alter ego, the young prince was in an unusually good mood.

"Did you lock me out just now?" Thomas called upward.

"Perceptive of you."

"That was a nasty trick."

"Locking the window against a thief? I should be given a medal!"

Pingree poked out from behind a column. "What's got into him?"

"Hush," said Rosetta.

"Must be those confidence-building exercises you've given him."

"I have as much right here as you!" Thomas replied, his face reddening.

Godric gave a glance at Rosetta, then hopped off the chandelier and twirled himself expertly to the floor. "Think about what you're saying, old man. I'm a prince. I live here. You're a thief. Admittedly, not a good one, but it's what you do. What gives you any rights at all?"

Thomas muttered something.

"What was that?"

"I said, some prince."

"What do you mean?"

"I mean you're a mad dog who goes about bashing himself in the head. You should be in the lunatic bin!"

"You'll take that back!" Godric cried.

Sylvie could hear the pain in his voice. Thomas had touched his weak spot.

"Never!" Thomas retorted.

"That's it, boy!" cried Riggeloff. "Slice his ears off!"

"Hit him! Poke him!" Pingree shrilled.

"Sylvie," whispered Rosetta, "do something!"

Whap!

Thomas had pulled a heavy glove from his pocket and slapped Godric's face with it. He then flung it to the floor. Of course, it didn't stay on the floor. "Pick it up!" he said in a threatening voice. The glove floated to the left. "Or fetch it!" He drew his sword from its scabbard. It made a loud scraping sound.

Pingree's face screwed into a grimace. "Oh, that grates!"

Thomas pulled back his arm and gave the air a great slice that shortened Godric's cloak by half a foot.

The prince unsheathed a silver sword of his own.

Pingree covered his ears. "A little oil, gentlemen," he cried. "A little oil!"

Godric floated in front of Thomas, trying to steady himself. Their swords clashed, but without gravity, the force of the blow threw the combatants in opposite directions.

Clang! Clangor! The rivals went at each other furiously.

"Stop it, both of you!" Sylvie cried, pushing off from the floor. Unable to slow down, she floated to the ceiling. She shoved herself from a roof beam and sailed past in the other direction, grabbing the edge of Godric's cloak. Pulled off balance, the prince failed to parry Thomas's thrust and took a cut on his forearm.

"First blood!" cried Riggeloff. "Now in for the kill!"

As Thomas swooped down, his blade glinting, Godric tried to free himself from Sylvie, but she refused to let go.

"Stop this, Godric!"

"Out of the way!"

At that moment the book was lifted roughly and yanked open. Instead of the roof beams of the great hall, there appeared dozens of lit dials and gauges and switches. The characters stopped what they were doing and stared.

"What's this?" It was a sharp male voice from somewhere.

"What's what?" A woman's voice.

"Oh, it's that stupid book. Remember?"

A young man's face appeared overhead. It was a handsome enough face, although the forehead looked pinched, as if when he was born, the doctor had held the forceps too tightly around his skull. He riffled through the pages. "The book from the capsule. The one that isn't Einstein."

A young woman appeared beside the man. Now, there was a pretty face, her forehead clear as a summer field. "Oh, yes!" She gave a little laugh. "We never figured out how it got in there."

"Shall I toss it in the compaction unit?"

"Let me read it first. We don't have a huge library up here."

"Okay, if you want to rot that pretty mind. Just chuck it when you're through." He gave her a frowning look. "So," he said, "the big guy treating you okay?"

"Matt? Sure."

"You're lucky. He's on my case all the time. I think he gets a kick out of it."

"Are we talking about the same guy?"

"You wouldn't see it. With you, he puts on the charm."

They didn't know it, of course, but half the cast of *The Great Good Thing* was staring up at them. Thomas and Godric had forgotten about their sword fight.

"So what's he do that's so terrible?" Kara said. "I mean, he's the commander. We all have our jobs."

"It's not the job. I can do my job in my sleep."

"Then what?"

Anger pinched his brow tighter. "How many times does he send you in to PAM?"

"Once a week, like always. I kind of enjoy it. It's a break."

He nodded. "He's sending me every other day, like I'm some kind of kook."

"Really?"

"Yesterday he had PAM give me a saliva test. We all know what *that's* about."

"Cortisol levels, right?"

"Do I look like a depressive personality to you?"

"You're . . . an interesting personality."

He gave a bitter laugh.

"Why don't you just talk to him about it?" she said.

"I don't have to."

"What's that mean?"

"Watch him. Watch how he is with you."

"With *me*?"

"That's right."

She sighed. "Okay, but now, if you don't mind, I'm going to go and *watch* some protein crystals. Maybe you've got something to do too."

"Yeah, I've got a hot date with PAM. We're checking sweat gland activity today."

Kara shook her head, and the book closed. When the backup lights came on, the king hurried in from the throne room. "What was *that*?"

"Sounds to me," said Rosetta, "like they're all getting a case of cabin fever."

"A case of what?" said the king, who had never been in a cabin.

"They've been stuck in this spaceship for a long time, maybe a year," Rosetta said, "with another year to go, not counting the return trip. I'd be cranky too."

"And who," said Sylvie, "is this Pam they keep talking about?"

"Yes," Rosetta said. "We haven't met her yet."

"What," King Walther interrupted, "was that fellow saying before? About 'chucking' something? I don't know that word."

"I think, Father," said Sylvie, "they're planning to throw our book away."

"What! Don't they know how much depends on it?"

"Well, *we* depend on it," said Sylvie, "but I don't suppose it means much to them."

"What will become of us?"

Sylvie hesitated. "Father, I don't like to bring this up, but what will become of us if they *don't* 'chuck' us? What if they put us back in that capsule?"

"I suppose we'll just keep on as before."

She waited for him to think his way through this, then saw that he wasn't able to. "Maybe you're right, Father," she said, giving him the best smile she could.

"We've come through worse than this," he said.

Sylvie was on the verge of replying when the roof of the castle again lifted away. The astronaut named Kara looked down briefly, then away. "So you don't mind?" she said to someone out of view.

"Go ahead," said a male voice. "We start the test at 0800. If we can get Mr. Winkermann to cooperate."

"Oh, he will," said Kara. "He'll complain, but he'll do it."

"I know. He's very good."

"But?"

"Let's leave it at that, Kara."

She nodded.

"He doesn't have to like it," the male voice added. "Or me."

Sylvie was watching Kara's face during this exchange. "I know," Kara said. "It's a shame though."

Matt's face, older than the others by some years, came into view. Smile lines mixed with thought lines. "Makes for a long trip, doesn't it?" he said.

"We're not even halfway there."

Matt raised a hand and touched Kara's hair. "Better take a little time now while you have the chance."

"Yeah. Actually, I can use the break."

"You all right?"

"I don't know what's going on. I've started forgetting things. Stupid things. Like yesterday I couldn't find my T-shirt. My yellow one? And now I'm missing my blue barrette."

"Oh!" Matt looked relieved. "Do you think we ought to alert Houston?"

"Ha-ha."

"Go," he said, "get out of here. Read your book."

Kara started the book from the beginning. It was good for the characters to have to get to their places and deliver their lines. It kept them from thinking about themselves so much. Prince Riggeloff stole the royal jewels; Sylvie sought safety inside the invisible fish; the priest healed the donkey's injured foot with his magic spell; Pingree told abominable jokes; the thieves turned into crickets; the Keeper of the Cave turned into handsome Prince Godric. For hours, as Kara lay in her space cot reading, Godric and Thomas didn't exchange a cross word.

But the Reader's mind was wandering. She read a page twice, as if she wasn't paying attention. That meant Sylvie and the others had to act out the scene again. Finally, after flipping back and forth, Kara laid the book down in the air in front of her, snapped off her light, and looked out the ship's window.

The book, still open, floated where she'd left it, just moving slightly with the currents of air-conditioning. Sylvie found herself watching the reflection of Kara's eyes, light blue, in the darkened window and, through that reflection, an explosive profusion of lights—of *stars*, Sylvie realized with a little gasp.

"Beautiful, isn't it?" said a quiet voice behind her.

"Fangl!" she said, startled. But she was glad he was there. Her geometry tutor knew so many things about life outside the book.

"You remember," he said, "when I told you there were more suns than just ours?"

"Those," she said in a shaky voice, "those are *suns*? There must be hundreds of them!"

"There are billons of them, Your Highness."

"That word isn't in the book. Is it very many?"

"Oh, yes."

"But they're so small."

He explained how large things could look small at a great distance. The distances, in this case, were unimaginable.

"Is that," she said, "what you call the universe?"

"It's part of it."

"Part of it!"

Sylvie stared at the reflection of Kara's eyes in the spaceship's window.

"What is it, Your Highness?"

She shook her head. "I had the strangest sensation just

then, Fangl. I imagined I was looking out through her eyes."

He smiled gently. "Do you want to see what she sees?"

"Yes, but not only that."

He waited.

Sylvie struggled with the unfamiliar feeling. "Don't you see? She's exploring the universe. She's actually doing it. I'm just . . . along for the ride."

"It's a fine ride, Your Highness."

"I know," she said. "I should be grateful."

He nodded. "You were written to do great good things, not watch other people do them."

"Is that very selfish?"

"It doesn't matter whether it is or not. It's your character."

"I suppose you're right. You generally are."

"You're the heroine of your story, Princess. You have to let this young woman be the heroine of hers."

Sylvie was silent.

He smiled. "Well, well."

"What?"

"It looks like our new Reader has fallen asleep."

Sylvie gazed at the side of Kara's face and at the awesome brilliance beyond.

"A heroine," Sylvie murmured. "Yes. I can see that."

chapter five

Over the next few days Kara read *The Great Good Thing* three and a half times and in fact attached the book with Velcro to the wall of her work space, where it waved gently, half-open, like an underwater plant.

It was a pleasant time. Characters in a book can tell how Readers feel about them. It has to do with the way they breathe, the way their eyes flick from one sentence to the next, the pressure of their hands as they hold the page. This Reader was a good one. Even the jester, who liked no one, began to refer to Kara by name.

Norbert Fangl, with his scientific bent, was particularly interested in Kara's experiments with protein crystals. From remarks Kara made to the other astronauts, Fangl learned that crystals grown on Earth are deformed by gravity, but they reach their perfect shape in space. Fangl loved shapes, especially "perfect" ones.

Other characters, like Laurel, liked looking at the plants Kara was growing, some of them for experiments, some for food. The smell of wheatgrass was exhilarating as it wafted through the pages. Then there were the animals: dozens of white mice, trays of earthworms, any number of insects. Kara took care of them all.

Although the characters liked Kara, they began to distrust her colleague, Jeff Winkermann.

"I thought you were going to chuck that," Wink said, interrupting her in the middle of the scene where Sylvie discovers the underwater entrance to Humped Mountain.

Kara looked up in surprise. "I may hang on to it. There are so few interesting things to read around here."

"Well, read the flight manual. You're starting to get sloppy."

"What!"

"During the power-down exercise? What were you thinking?"

"I was thinking exactly what I was supposed to be thinking!"

"You kept glancing out the window. What were you looking for? Seagulls?"

"What were *you* doing watching me?"

He gave a dismissive laugh. "Don't you think you're worth looking at?"

"Wink, don't start."

"Start what?"

"Look, there are three of us in this tin can. We've got to live together."

His face came into view above the book. To Sylvie he didn't look as handsome as before. "You don't seem to mind *him* looking at you."

"What are you talking about?"

"Those cozy little scenes outside the sleeping quarters. The press of a hand. The meaningful look."

"Wink, this mission is too important to jeopardize. Matt knows that better than anyone. You should too."

"Oh, I don't know. A little romance sounds pretty good just about now."

"Quit it."

"Oh, you'd rather read that stupid book. Come on. What do you say?"

"Please let go of my arm."

"Hey!" Pingree called out suddenly. He'd been watching from the west turret. "Leave her alone!"

Godric shouted up at them. "Unhand her, you worm!"

Princess Sylvie looked around, amazed at how many characters were looking up. They were all disobeying the first rule of fictional characters: Never, ever, look at the Reader; and no one was correcting them.

Kara tapped a little wire that was poking up by her chin. "Matt," she said, "could you come up here? We've got a problem."

Wink glared. "Okay!" His face disappeared for a few seconds, then reappeared. Suddenly the characters were thrown around violently. Pingree even fell off the turret and landed in a bush. "I'll just chuck this out for you," the young man said.

"Leave my book *alone*!"

But it snapped closed, and the characters could hear and see no more. The tumbling about continued, however. They spun wildly and then lurched to a sickening stop.

Silence. The backup lights sputtered and came on. Slowly, the characters picked themselves up. Pingree rubbed his bony hip.

Sylvie caught sight of her friend Laurel. "I don't like this," she said.

Her friend with the dark blue eyes usually had a solution to the problems that arose in the kingdom. This time she was frowning.

A herald came running by and then, from the opposite direction, a royal courier. Their message was the same: King Walther desired to meet with everyone in the throne room immediately.

Sylvie and Laurel went in together, finding the place packed with the book's characters, even the most minor. Many held on to the network of guide ropes; others floated an inch or two off the floor. At the front sat Queen Emmeline, with her dog Lulu tied on her lap with a ribbon.

The king held up a hand for silence. "Thank you, dear Subjects, Verbs, and Objects, for coming at such short notice," he began, "but we are faced with an emergency."

The reeve nudged a muttering peasant and held his finger to his lips. The hall quieted.

"It appears that we're to be . . . chucked."

Murmurs broke out in the crowd.

"Wot's 'ee say?" said Ursula, the fish woman, to the apple seller.

"Chopped, I think 'ee said."

"I don't blame you for not knowing the word," the

king went on. "According to the royal grammarian, it means we're being . . ." He faltered. "That is, we're, well, being thrown out."

"Thrown out, he says?"

"Wot?"

"Discarded," the king went on, "tossed in the trash, emptied with the chamber pot."

A confused hubbub broke out in various parts of the hall, and it took the bellowing lungs of the Chief Councillor to restore quiet.

"We don't know if this will really happen," the king continued, "or what form our 'chucking' might take. But I wanted to bring you together, while time remains, so you could prepare yourselves." The silence became absolute now.

"Hear, hear!" the king's guards suddenly shouted. Of course, that was all they ever said.

"Hain't you the king?" shouted a belligerent thief named McGettigan. "You're supposed to protect us!"

A chambermaid raised a timorous hand. "Excusin' Your Highness," she began, "but how can a great and fair kingdom, stretchin' from west to north and containing a good-size forest besides . . ." She looked around her. "How can all this be tossed out?"

"Hear, hear!"

"What monster would be huge enough to do this?" called out the royal slipper-maker.

The king waited for silence. "A Reader," he said simply.

"A Reader!" the crowd whispered, one to another.

"Surely not that luvly girl we been seein' these past days," the cook's portly wife called out.

"No, not Kara," said King Walther.

"She's a good'n," called the woodcutter.

Prince Godric stood up. "I thought they were our friends," he said. "For a Reader to turn against a book . . ." He shook his head. "It's unnatural!"

In the midst of the cross talk Sylvie heard her name whispered. It was her dark-eyed friend Laurel. "Let's go outside," the girl said.

They slipped into the corridor, then out to the court-yard, with the peddlers' stalls and cages of chickens.

"Do you really think he'll do this?" Sylvie said.

"He could. Readers are ever so much larger than books."

"Can we stop him?"

Laurel was watching a three-legged dog nosing about the cheese stall.

"Couldn't we enter his dream or something," Sylvie continued, "and talk to him inside his head? We've done that with some Readers."

"I know. But first they have to be reading our story; and then they have to dream about it. This fellow hasn't done either."

"We can't just give up!"

Laurel sighed. "I wish we knew more about space-ships. How do they dispose of things they don't want? If they incinerate their trash . . ."

"What's that mean?"

"Burn it."

"Don't say that!" Sylvie shivered. A distant memory flashed through her mind, of a boy who had once set fire to the pages of the book.

"We might also be shredded."

"Laurel!"

"Or vented out into space. They've got to do something. There's not going to be a trash pickup for another three years."

The girls were silent for a time.

Then Sylvie said, in a wondering voice, "What was it he said? Is there a word *compaction*?"

"He said that?"

"What does it mean?"

"Do you really want to know?"

Sylvie nodded.

"It means we're to be crushed to death."

The girls looked at each other with horror. Without a word, they turned and went back inside the castle.

Time passed. No one knew how much. The book remained closed, but it *remained*. Somehow it had escaped destruction. Each day the book continued to exist felt like a gift. Little things didn't matter to Sylvie so much. When Pingree groused about how unreasonable the queen was being, Sylvie told him to enjoy life a little more.

"Enjoy? I'm surrounded by dolts and tyrants!"

"Pingree, have you ever just sat and looked at the illustration of Humped Mountain?"

"Why would I do that?"

"You should. Life is precious. Wake up and smell the pages."

As weeks turned to months old rivalries began to resurface—particularly between Prince Godric and the thief Thomas. Queen Emmeline became her overbearing self again, and Riggeloff found lots to get angry about. One good thing came from their long neglect: Everyone became proficient at gliding. It wasn't really flying; they had to push off from some surface every few seconds. But if they ever did get a Reader again, they could whiz right through the story.

Then, one morning, a strange and upsetting thing occurred: The great tortoise disappeared. At first Sylvie thought the creature must have wandered off into the forest (it was quite a large tract of land, much of it unexplored). But the tortoise had always come back before and would let Sylvie feed it eucalyptus leaves and then allow her to climb on its back for a ride. It was incomprehensible to think someone would steal the beast or that anyone *could*. As days went by Princess Sylvie grew more upset. On the fourth day she woke up to find a note propped by her bedside table:

IF YOU WANT TO SEE YOUR YOU-KNOW-WHAT AGAIN, YOU MUST AGREE TO DO EXACTLY AS I SAY.

LEAVE YOUR ANSWER BEHIND THE SUIT OF ARMOR IN THE THRONE ROOM.

-A FRIEND

Sylvie read the note several times. Who would take her beloved tortoise and then have the nerve to sign the note *A Friend*? What kind of friend was this?

Well, she was certainly not going to agree to blackmail. Besides, she was sure she'd find the tortoise if she just kept looking. The creature was ten feet across! She wrote back:

> *If you are such a friend, you will bring back my tortoise. If you are not my friend, you are in grandiloquent trouble.*

She didn't know what that meant exactly, but probably no one else did either. The big word was one of the puffy adjectives she liked to rest her head on when taking her afternoon nap. She signed the note politely:

> *Sincerely,*
> *Princess Sylvie, Daughter of the Realm*

She thought awhile, then added:

> *P.S. The tortoise needs his eucalyptus leaves every evening, and his shell should be oiled every three days.*

She closed the envelope with the royal seal and left it behind the armor, as instructed. Next morning it was gone.

Not waiting for a response, Sylvie searched everywhere she could think of. She explored the most brambly part of the forest; she even climbed inside the invisible fish and rode to the bottom of the Mere to examine the underwater entrance to Humped Mountain.

No tortoise.

"He's got to be somewhere!" she cried to Laurel as they sat on a rock by the Mere.

"That is true. Everything is somewhere."

"This is the meanest thing I ever heard of!"

Laurel, although just Sylvie's age, had a look that was much older. "You know," she said, "we *will* find your tortoise. This is a book. There is no exit from a book."

Sylvie was not good at being patient, but within the hour, something happened that took her mind off the tortoise entirely. The kingdom shook and swayed, causing the Mere of Remind to slosh waves high onto the shore; and then, amazingly, the sky lifted away and the book opened.

A tear fell onto the page three lines below where Sylvie stood. Kara's face was above her. Another tear fell.

The characters who were needed for that page had all gathered, ready to reenact the story, but Kara wasn't looking at the words.

"What happened?" came a man's voice.

"He . . ." Kara could hardly speak. "He destroyed my plants."

"What!"

"Many of them. Some of our food crops. A lot of the experiments . . ."

"Good God!" Matt's stricken face appeared above the book.

She nodded at the tiny microphone in front of his mouth. "Let's turn that off a minute."

"Right," he said.

"Are we private now?"

"He can't hear us."

"Well," she said in a whisper, "we know he's jealous of you. And he's kind of obsessed with me."

"Obsessed?"

She paused. "I don't know what else to call it."

"Kara, we've just gone into orbit. We're a day away from landing on a moon of Jupiter! Why would he pull a stunt like this?"

Kara looked around. "He's down in the landing module, right?"

"Yeah, getting things stowed and ready."

"Well," Kara whispered, "do you remember this book?"

Matt looked down into the kingdom. "The fairy story. Yes. Been a while."

"He snatched it away from me a long time ago. He said he was tossing it in the compaction unit."

"And?"

"I thought he had. But I just found it in a box in the bottom of his sleep container."

"What's that got to do—?"

"There were other things in there." She held up a test tube with fibers in it.

"What's that?"

"If I had to bet, I'd say it's a sample of my hair."

"I don't get it."

"Look at these other things." She held up a yellow T-shirt, an eyebrow pencil, a blue barrette, and several other objects that Sylvie could not make out. "Yes," said Kara, looking into Matt's face, "they all belong to me."

"He's made a . . . ," Matt began. "A sort of . . ."

"Shrine?" whispered Kara.

Matt gave her a long look. "Let's get him up here."

"What are you going to do?"

But he had already turned on the intercom. "Wink, we need you up here on the double." He paused, listening. "Never mind about that now," he said sharply. "We'll do it later."

Kara and Matt exchanged a look while they waited for Wink to appear.

"So what is it that couldn't wait?" The young astronaut lurched into view, then stopped short, seeing the book and other objects in Kara's hands.

"We've got a few questions for you," Matt said, his voice steady.

Jeff Winkermann tipped his head to the side and looked at his two shipmates through narrowed eyes.

Kara held the objects up. "Care to comment?"

He raised his eyebrows, considering. "I don't think so."

"You don't *think* so?" Kara said.

Wink pursed his lips in thought. "Nope."

Sylvie, looking up from the page, could see Kara's furious look.

"Except," he said, "what the devil were you doing going through my things?"

"*Your* things?"

"What do you have to say about Kara's experiments?" Matt said quietly.

"That I can explain." He looked from one to the other. "An accident, totally. I wasn't watching where I was going and knocked against a couple of trays of stuff. Anything damaged?"

Kara took in Wink's look of wide-eyed innocence. "Two years of work," she said slowly.

"You mean those few little . . . ?"

"Fortunately, you missed some plants; and the trays of protein crystals were in the other compartment. I found the mice floating around the cabin, some alive, some not."

"Wink," said Matt very quietly, "I would throw you in the brig, except we don't have a brig. I would relieve you of duty, except it takes all three of us to fly this thing. So my options are limited. I will tell you, though, that when we get back home, you will face charges."

"Charges!" Wink made a sour face. "For what? Bumping into vegetables?"

"The main problem," said Kara, trying to keep her voice even, "is that you damaged the diodes."

"I did what?"

"You know the greenhouse uses light-emitting diodes as its light source."

"I don't know. I guess so."

"If we can't fix them, you can forget about fresh vegetables for the next two years."

"I'm sorry, okay?"

"I don't believe it was an accident," said Matt.

"Prove it, hotshot!" Wink's eyes flared.

Sylvie could see Matt's jaw clenching and unclenching.

"Go on!" Pingree yelled up from the page. "Pop him one!"

"Why don't you go on down and finish your work on the LEM," Matt said at last. "We need to get the lunar excursion module in shape."

"Sounds like an idea." The young man jumped down through a hatch and disappeared.

Matt looked at Kara. "I'm not real comfortable about tomorrow," he said. "I'll be up here orbiting while he's with you down on the surface."

"What do you think he'll do?" she said.

"That depends on how crazy he is."

"Somehow I don't think PAM is going to solve this problem for us."

"Hasn't so far," Matt said.

"He used to be such a great guy. Remember how he'd make us laugh?"

"Two years can do strange things to you. The results from PAM aren't clear. It may be some sort of late-onset bipolar disorder."

"Didn't we all go through batteries of tests before the mission started?"

"Some things don't show up. That's why we have the Performance and Affect Monitor."

"It's got to be painful being him."

"Kara," Matt said, then seemed to falter.

"What?"

He gave her a serious smile. "You be careful."

She nodded.

"I mean it," he said. "You're going to be out there alone with him."

"Yeah," she said. "No kidding."

He touched her hair lightly, then disappeared from view.

chapter six

It was early evening, and Sylvie paced back and forth on the lookout tower of the castle's keep. She was at the highest point she could get to, as if that would bring her closer to events in the spaceship. The astronauts—two of them, anyway—were soon to land on the moon of another planet, and here Sylvie was stuck inside a book. Never had she felt so dissatisfied with her story, with its quaint plot and old-fashioned illustrations.

"You're the heroine of your story, Princess. You have to let this young woman be the heroine of hers." She remembered Fangl's words, but they brought no comfort.

Was she imagining things, or was there a bit more gravity now? Suddenly her world gave a lurch. Sylvie fell to the stone parapet and bruised her elbow. Fell! Before, she would have had to *will* herself down, using Rosetta's breathing techniques.

Fangl poked his head up through the hole in the trapdoor at the top of the tower. "May I join you, Your Highness?" he said, stepping from the ladder.

"So you're curious too?"

"Immensely."

"Did you feel that lurch a minute ago?"

"Rocket thrusters, I would think. But whether they're on the ship or the landing module, I have no idea."

"If only the book would open!"

"I know! No one has ever been this far from Earth before. If I overheard correctly, we're actually circling one of the moons of Jupiter!"

"I'm afraid I don't know what that is."

"Jupiter? It's a huge planet in the outer reaches of the solar system. It has scores of moons, four of them quite large."

Sylvie tried to imagine such a thing, but she knew little about life outside her book. "Did you notice, Fangl, that we have more gravity now? I actually fell down."

"Yes. More gravity or more velocity."

"You keep saying things I don't understand."

"I mean, Princess, that if we suddenly speed up or suddenly slow down, it will *feel* like gravity. Well, it *is* gravity in a way."

"I see. I think."

"Maybe the rockets just changed our speed."

"You are such a smart one!" Sylvie said. "You make me almost understand you."

From her vantage point, Sylvie could see a lower balcony on which the queen was taking the evening air with her maid and a male servant. Queen Emmeline was very sensitive to noises and sudden vibrations—anything that disturbed her world.

Looking farther down, Sylvie watched the peddlers,

diminished by distance, selling their wares as usual while several ladies entered a coach, a footman holding the door for them. To the east lay the Mere of Remind, a body of water as dangerous as it was lovely. On the shore she could just make out two young men. She looked closer. They were fighting! Hitting each other and falling down.

"Do you see that?" she cried.

"Is that the young prince?"

"Yes, and Thomas. I suppose they're fighting over Rosetta."

"Interesting."

"Interesting? It's horrible!"

"Yes, of course." They watched in silence. "Does it strike you as odd, Princess, at the moment when humanity is about to do a miraculous thing, setting foot for the first time on a world hundreds of millions of miles away from Earth, that people are still interested in punching one another in the nose?"

"It's depressing." She squinted into the distance. "What are they doing now?"

Fangl reached for the telescope mounted on the castellated wall. He looked through it briefly before passing it to Sylvie.

"Oh no!" she said. The fight had taken an unfortunate turn. Prince Godric would throw a punch at Thomas and then, in the next moment, would hit himself in the stomach or give himself an uppercut to the chin.

"It's not fair!" she cried. "It's two against one!"

It was true. The dark half of Godric's nature had

joined forces with Thomas and was helping to beat the young prince senseless.

"Call the guards, Fangl! Quick, we've got to stop this!"

"Certainly, Your High—" He never finished. In fact, nobody finished anything, because at that moment a violent earthquake threw all the characters, from Godric to the coachman, to the ground. Sylvie heard her mother's scream as the sky tore open and a freezing shadow covered the kingdom, accompanied by a loud hissing sound, like static. Coldness seized Sylvie's bones. She shivered uncontrollably, and old Fangl, skinny as he was, shivered harder. Even more terrifying, a great puffy creature with a mirror for a face appeared overhead and glared down at them.

A muffled shout from above: "Hey, let's put this in the capsule, eh, Kara?"

"Don't you dare!" It was Kara's voice from somewhere nearby, and it, too, was strangely muffled.

"Wouldn't that be rich?" came the mocking voice. "A thousand years from now some alien comes across our capsule in the ice of Mount Pwyll."

"Give that to me, Wink!"

"He opens it and finds some fruity story about knights and ladies!"

"Just give it to me!"

A thick white object reached overhead. An arm, Sylvie realized.

"You want it? Go get it!"

With that, the book went spinning off through

space. "Whoa!" cried Sylvie, her stomach clenching. She grabbed on to a metal wall bracket as glaring light radiated her world and the book whirled like a mad merry-go-round. It didn't slow down for a long time. She wondered if she'd skitter right off this freezing globe into the depths of space. *Poor Mother*, she thought briefly, remembering how the slightest thing upset her.

At last the spinning began to slow, and the true terror of the situation came home to her. They had escaped being "compacted" and escaped being stuffed in a container and buried on a frozen moon at the far end of the solar system. Instead, it was their fate to lie completely exposed on that same icy world and shake with cold for eternity. The atmosphere, whatever it was made of, was filled with an endless crackling and hissing. She glanced around as the moonscape came into focus. What she saw were icy plains with deep scratches along the surface, like broken glass that had healed itself with an ooze of glue. Was this their home now—this frozen hell? Where were the villages? Where were the sheep and birds and castles and . . . and people?

The book, rotating slowly, touched the ice, lifted away, and touched down again, sliding for long seconds before coming to rest. The pages stood up like an open fan before gradually subsiding.

The cold was shocking, and Sylvie glanced with pity at Fangl, who was slumped against the wall shaking violently. "F-Fangl?" she managed to say.

The geometer just shook his head, too cold to speak.

Sylvie looked down from the parapet. The peddlers and court ladies had all fled into the castle. On the slope of Humped Mountain a small herd of sheep huddled together, their wool white with frost. Thomas and Godric, their fight forgotten, were rolling on the ground with their clothing wrapped tightly around them.

"Sylvie?" said a calm voice just behind her.

Princess Sylvie spun around. It was her friend Laurel, and she was smiling. Even stranger, she didn't appear in the least cold!

"L-L-Laurel! Thank God! Are you all right?"

The girl lifted her arms, opening the edges of her thick blue cloak. "Come," she said.

Sylvie gratefully ducked under the cloak. To her amazement she found it warm. "Oh, this is wonderful!" she cried.

"Let's get Mr. Fangl in too," said the girl with the dark blue eyes.

Sylvie helped Norbert Fangl to his feet. It was like picking up an armful of sticks.

"Th-Thank you," said the geometer, slipping in on the other side of Laurel. His quaking gradually subsided. "This is remarkable," he said at last. The scientist in him plucked at the material, trying to understand what it was made of. "How," he said, "is this possible?"

She smiled. "An author has some say about her wardrobe."

"I suppose that's true."

"When I came into the book, I just wrote down what I thought I'd need."

"Including a cloak that would always keep you warm."

"And cool in summer."

Princess Sylvie was listening to the odd, inhuman whistles and peeps that punctuated the background hiss. "What are those sounds?" she said.

"I have a guess," said Fangl, cocking his head. "I'd say it's the radiation coming from Jupiter. It's pretty intense. Even in their heavy suits, the astronauts probably can't stay outside very long."

Sylvie decided not to ask him what he was talking about. Instead, she looked gratefully at her two friends. Laurel stood in the center, her cloak raised like blue wings around the shoulders of the others. Sylvie's forehead ached with cold and her hair whitened with frost, but the center of her body was warm beneath the amazing cloak.

"Sylvie," said Laurel breathlessly, "look up."

"Oh!" exclaimed the princess, lifting her eyes to an enormous orange ball, with swirls and dark discolorations, surrounded by vast white bands of ammonia clouds. It took up nearly half the sky! Off to the left, edging into darkness, the heavens glimmered, with one star brighter than the rest.

"Is that the sun, Mr. Fangl?" said Laurel, nodding toward the star.

"Yes, that would be Sol. Too far away to send much warmth."

"And above us . . . ?"

"Jupiter. We are on one of its moons. There's another," he said, pointing to a copper-colored ball floating in the distance. "And another."

Laurel gave a little sigh and threw her head back, as if to take in everything at once. Sylvie was doing the same. She didn't know why, but a great surge of feeling swept through her, bringing tears to her eyes. In seconds the tears turned to crystal.

"It's so beautiful!"

"Somehow I've seen this before," Laurel whispered.

"How could that be?"

"Centuries and centuries ago. I know it's impossible," Laurel continued. "We didn't exist then. But I *feel* we did."

"Out here," Fangl said, "anything seems possible. You'd almost believe time could go backward."

"If we die out here . . . ," Sylvie began.

"You can't die, Sylvie," Laurel corrected her gently. "You're fictional."

"What I mean is, if we don't get back home . . ." She didn't finish her thought immediately. A shooting star disappeared around the curve of Jupiter.

"Yes?" Laurel said.

"It might be . . . all right."

"I've never seen the constellations so bright," said Fangl.

"Constellation?" said Sylvie, still staring up. "What's that again?"

"A constellation is—well, look up to the right. Do you see the outline of a drinking cup?" He pointed. "Those stars would be the handle, and—"

Laurel gently laid her hand on Fangl's arm. "What do *you* see, Princess Sylvie?" she said.

Sylvie cast wide eyes across the firmament. She was silent for several seconds. "Maybe I'm wrong."

"You can't be."

"Well, what I see . . ." She paused again. "Yes, it's a woman, flying."

"Where?" said Laurel.

"See that bright star there?" She pointed.

"That would be Capella," Fangl said, squinting.

"Shh, let her be."

"That's her feet. And then, you see that line of stars? Those are her arms spread out."

"Oh, yes," said Fangl.

"And her head is that bright star just beyond."

Fangl nodded. "Well," he said, "you've made a new combination."

"A new constellation, you mean," Laurel said. "What should we call it?"

Sylvie didn't answer. She was smiling up at the flying woman.

Fangl cleared his throat. "How about the constellation of Sylvie?"

"Oh, I don't think so," said Sylvie. "It's about much more than me."

"Of course," said Fangl, "but you saw the pattern. That's all a constellation is—a way of seeing things."

"I like your way of seeing things, Sylvie," Laurel murmured.

"I don't think," said Fangl quietly, "I'll ever look at Perseus and Auriga the same way again." He lowered his eyes to the horizon. Beyond the margins of the book lay the blinding expanse of the moon they were stranded on. No sign of life. "What's that, Your Highness?" he said, pointing.

In the distance Sylvie could just make out a dot of silver. It was coming toward them over the ice.

"Let's have a look with that telescope, Fangl," said Sylvie. "It looks like a carriage of some kind."

"You're right!" Fangl exclaimed. "It's some sort of moon buggy. They must have brought it with them in the module."

"Oh, dear," Sylvie said, squinting through the instrument. "One of those horrible fat creatures is driving it!"

Laurel got a look through the telescope. "It's all right. It's just someone inside a space suit."

"I think it's Kara!" cried Sylvie, taking another turn at the telescope.

The astronaut was struggling to control the moon rover and bring it to a stop in light gravity on ice. It slid past, coming to rest thirty yards farther on. Very slowly, Kara turned the vehicle around. Finally she lost patience and jumped out. Jumping out meant bounding twenty feet into the nonexistent atmosphere and gradually coming down to the surface. Her attempts to run were equally odd. It was like watching someone running under water. At last she reached the book and picked it up, holding it carefully.

"Thank goodness!" she said. Then: "What? Yes, I'm coming. Yes, I *know* we've got a lot to do. If you hadn't thrown the book in the first place . . ."

Sylvie gave Fangl a puzzled look.

"She's talking to that other one," he said quietly.

"But he's not here."

"Microphone," he said, "in her suit." He smiled at her confusion. "I'll explain later."

"Yes, yes." Even muffled, Kara's voice sounded angry. "You just get the capsule ready. I'll be there."

The book closed, and the air within it grew suddenly warmer. *Oh,* thought Sylvie, *that feels good. Whatever happens now, at least we're not freezing.*

There was a new problem, though. The kingdom had begun shaking violently.

"The moon buggy!" cried Fangl, hugging the castle wall to keep his balance.

"Bumpy ride!" Laurel called out.

Because of the light gravity and broken terrain, the book kept jogging open, allowing in gusts of frigid air and scraps of talk. Sylvie didn't understand much of it, since it had to do with longitude and drilling depths.

"Yes, I see you," Kara called out finally. "I'm applying the aerobrakes. Yeah, well, I'd like to see *you* do this!"

Sylvie's stomach dropped as her world swerved in a semicircle and bumped to a stop. The book stayed mostly closed until the buggy started again. Now both astronauts were in it. Sylvie soon found herself tilting backward. Even Humped Mountain was tilting. Several sheep lost their footing and rolled down its slope. The kingdom straightened out finally—apparently, they'd reached a plateau—and then the sound of drilling found its way in through the loosely closed pages.

"Let's pop that baby in there," said Wink.

"Aren't we going to say a few words?" said Kara.

"Hail and farewell?"

"No, no, let me say something. It's not every century our country leaves a capsule on another world."

"As if anybody's ever going to find it."

"You don't know that."

"Or make sense of it."

"Do you *mind*? Okay, I just want to say—let's see—it's an incredible honor to be here in this amazing place. And, and . . . Wait! I know. There's a description in *The Great Good Thing*."

"Kara, for God's sake!"

Intense coldness swept over the pages containing the first description of Humped Mountain.

"Here it is." She cleared her throat. "'There was something alien about the place, the raw stone of the mountain rising out of the Mere like an angry fist. Sylvie would stare at it often from her perch on the opposite shore, as if it were a closed box containing a secret. She didn't know what the secret was, but—'"

"Could we hurry this up?"

"Keep your shirt on! '—but she would not rest till she had discovered it, for it was the key to everything. There would be no peace in the kingdom, she knew, unless—'"

"Okay, that's enough. We've got to start loading."

"Wink, you are awful."

"You're just finding that out?"

"But wasn't that a wonderful description?"

"Sure, yeah."

The violent bumping and veering began again.

Finally they came to a stop. The pages barely touched one another, and from the top of one page, where the corner had been turned down, Sylvie could see brilliant slivers of moonlight. She led her friends there, and they lay along the top line of print and peered out.

They could see nothing definite. What they heard, mostly, was a pounding of machinery and the crackling of ice. Then came a different kind of commotion, like the roar of hard objects sliding down a chute.

"Mr. Fangl," Sylvie whispered, "what is going on?"

"I'm not sure. They spoke of gathering samples. Of ice, I presume."

"Yes."

"But listen to all this," he said, tilting his head. "It's more than collecting samples. They're loading in a cargo."

"Mysterious."

"Very," Fangl agreed.

After some time the moon vehicle was driven into a dark place. The slamming of a hatch door reverberated through the kingdom, and then Wink's distant voice was heard shouting, "Four minutes, Kara. You better move it!"

Sylvie looked at Fangl. "Four minutes until what?"

Fangl shook his head.

The answer came soon enough.

"Ignite engines!" Wink shouted.

There was a violent vibration.

"We have ignition!" Kara sang out.

"Ten seconds to liftoff! Nine, eight, seven . . ."

"I think, Your Highness," said Fangl, "it might be a good idea to hang on to something."

Sylvie held the hem of Laurel's remarkable cloak, and Laurel reached her arm around *adamant*, the closest big word she could find. Surely words wouldn't fly off a page, no matter how a book was shaken—especially a word like *adamant*.

The vibration increased, filling the kingdom. That was followed by a feeling of intense compression. Indeed, the force of gravity actually bent some of the taller letters and held the covers so tightly closed that not even a Reader could have opened them.

They were back in space.

chapter seven

When the pressure eased up a bit, Sylvie forced herself onto her elbow and called to her father.

"I'm here, on the next page!"

The pressure on Sylvie's body was lessening by the moment, and soon she was able to stand, though it felt as if she had lead weights in her shoes. "Where's Mother?" she said when she'd reached the king. "Have you seen her?"

King Walther hesitated. "She hasn't taken these recent events very well, I'm afraid."

"I should go see her."

"She may not talk to you. She hasn't spoken a word to anyone since . . ."

Sylvie waited for him to find the words. She found she often had to wait.

"It was a terrible thing," he went on, "when that man threw us out into space, and the Great Cold came. Your mother . . . Well, go see her," he said. "Maybe you can bring her back."

"Back from where?"

"I wish I knew."

Laurel took Sylvie's arm, and together they climbed the spiral staircase. By now the pull of gravity had lessened to nearly zero, and they found they needed to hold the guide ropes. A guard stood outside the queen's chamber, anchoring himself by holding the latch. He nodded and swung the door open.

The sight of her mother, under mounds of tightly tucked blankets in the oversized bed, nicked Sylvie's heart. She looked so small and frail. "Mother? It's me. Sylvie."

Queen Emmeline's face was blank.

Sylvie signaled to the lady's maid, the plump one who'd been with the queen on the balcony. "You're Mary, aren't you? Can you tell us what happened?"

The girl looked frightened. She ran her hand back and forth nervously along one of the guide ropes, as if polishing it.

"It's all right, Mary," Laurel said.

"Well," she began, "when that awful creature come, you know, with the fat arms and a mirror for a face, and lookin' down at us bold as brass, I thought we was done for." She shook her head at the memory.

"Go on," Sylvie said.

"And then the cold!"

"Yes, it got terribly cold."

Mary stole a pitying glance at the queen. "But she'd have pulled through even that."

"What was it, then?"

"The looking up."

"The what?"

"There's a reason for that rule in the kingdom about not looking up. Now I know why." Mary glanced at the ceiling to demonstrate.

"What did she *see?*" Sylvie was becoming exasperated.

Mary whispered: *"Nothing!"*

"Nothing?"

"Everything!" Mary gestured helplessly.

"I don't understand."

"Ah . . . ah . . . ," the queen cried out, hearing them speak.

"It's all right, Mother," said Sylvie, stroking her arm.

"Maybe," said Laurel, "we should get out of earshot."

The three young women stepped out on the balcony.

"Obviously," Sylvie said quietly, "she was terrified by something."

"So wouldn't you be," returned Mary with indignation, "if you'd been brought up proper, with a nice little moon and three clouds always overhead."

"It wasn't that nice little moon this time, was it?" Laurel said.

"No indeed!" Mary held to the balustrade. "To look up and see that big bloody-looking planet about to crush the life out of you! Sweet heavens! And beyond that, those awful stars stretching out and out without no end to 'em."

"I see," Laurel said. She laid a hand on the girl's shoulder. "Thank you, Mary. Keep watch over her now, won't you?"

"I will, miss."

When the friends were alone in the corridor, Sylvie said, "What do you think?"

"I think," said Laurel carefully, "she saw what we saw. What I mean is, she had a glimpse beyond the book."

"To me it was so beautiful!" Sylvie said, letting her feet lift off the floor so she could float down the corridor.

"Strange, isn't it? The same universe shining over us all, yet she saw something cold and terrifying, and we saw . . ."

"Yes," Sylvie said quietly. "I could have stayed out there forever, just to look up."

"We almost did."

"I know," Sylvie said soberly. "Don't think I'm not grateful for that wonderful cloak of yours."

They glided out a window and willed themselves to the ground. The apple seller was lashing down a length of canvas to keep his wares from floating off. He gave the princess a nod and reached under for two apples, one for each girl.

"Thanks!" Sylvie took a loud bite and looked up at the blue, storybook sky of their daytime scenes. "I wonder where we are now."

"On the way back to Earth, I'd think," Laurel said, polishing the apple on her hip. She gave a little wave and set out to find Fangl while the princess headed to the cliff overlooking the Mere. It was her favorite spot, and a perfect day, as always; but instead of bright sunlight on calm water, splinters of color darted in all directions, as if a rainbow had shattered. Sylvie understood what it was. In minimal gravity the waterfall no longer fell straight down from Humped Mountain, but spread outward in a curve, forming a skin of water overhead. The sun shot through it as through a prism, creating wild refractions.

She decided to climb down to the shore and visit her invisible fish. It would cheer her to take a ride in its stomach and see how the colored lights looked through its transparent sides. Standing at the water's edge, her blue shoes in the wet sand, she called to it.

No response.

Come to think, it hadn't been there yesterday either. The Mere was wide and the fish was, well, invisible, but it especially liked the cove and would heave its back out of the water, creating a wash of waves. Often the fish would circle close, and if she waded out a bit, would rub against her legs.

"Fish! Fish!" she called. Her voice echoed back from the mountain.

She climbed onto her usual rock, hoping to see better. A flutter of white caught her eye. To her surprise it was an envelope with her name on it. She felt a chill go through her when she saw the printing.

THIS IS YOUR SECOND CHANCE,

the note began.

IF YOU WANT TO SEE YOUR FISH OR TORTOISE AGAIN, COME ALONE AT MIDNIGHT TO THE WEST TURRET.

Again it was signed *A Friend.*

Sylvie stared at the words. Her second magical animal, even bigger than the tortoise, had been kidnapped. Unbelievable!

Her first thought was to show the note to Laurel; but then she remembered that the shepherdess Rosetta lived just up the hill. Sylvie found her out in back of her hut, picking watercress by the stream.

Rosetta wiped her wet hands on her dress. "Remember when we were online and nothing tasted like anything?" she said.

Sylvie nodded. "I remember you gave me a sandwich."

"A virtual watercress sandwich."

"I tried to be polite."

"You'll like this better," she said, taking a fresh loaf from a hamper and slicing it carefully.

The two friends sat on a wooden bench beside the stream. They tried passing a ladle of cold water between them, but the water kept floating away or hovering out of reach like a jellyfish. Rosetta jumped up and attempted to drink the water directly from the air. Princess Sylvie sputtered with laughter.

"It feels good to laugh again," she said.

"Yes," Rosetta agreed, drying her face. "I'm not getting a lot of laughs myself, with these crazy men fighting over me. Am I supposed to be impressed?"

"I suppose you could see it as a compliment."

"Violence as a compliment?"

They fell silent.

"So," said Rosetta, "any trace of the tortoise?"

Sylvie pulled the new message from the envelope. "I found another letter," she said.

"Uh-oh." Rosetta read it twice. "I suppose Riggeloff is behind this."

"That's what I'm thinking."

"He's mean enough."

They agreed there was no point in telling Sylvie's father. He'd send out his knights in five different directions, and they'd clump around for a while and scare the chipmunks. There was no way out, Sylvie decided. She'd have to meet the kidnapper.

"Not by yourself," said Rosetta firmly.

"I have to! It said in the letter."

"I don't care if it told you to stand on your head."

Sylvie agreed to let Rosetta come to the turret, but only if she'd keep hidden and not step out on the ramparts. That way, if Sylvie ran into trouble, Rosetta would be there to help.

"I don't like it," Rosetta said, "but I suppose it's useless to argue."

"Completely."

Rosetta watched as Sylvie stood up. "Well, I'd better get going," the princess said.

"What are you going to do?"

"Keep looking." Sylvie gave a sharp whistle, and before long the owl could be seen batting his way toward them over the trees.

"Maybe I'll check around the moat," Rosetta said.

"Good idea."

The owl arrived and, after several tries, scooped

the princess up and hoisted her over the trees.

"Tonight!" Rosetta called after her. She saw Sylvie nod and give a little wave before she was lost in the distance.

The king's forest was extensive but not endless. At a certain point the trees simply stopped, replaced by a narrow strip of white, like a sidewalk. Beyond that was nothing. Not an ordinary nothing, which is the absence of something. This nothing repelled the mind, and people's thoughts naturally turned away from it. Sylvie was the only character who'd ever crossed this boundary, and only when a Reader happened to dream about the story. Then Sylvie could cross into the dream. There was no dream for her today, so she and the owl stayed within the kingdom, crisscrossing the forest, swooping low over any ponds or brambly places that might conceal a large animal. It was exhausting, and the leather harness bit into Sylvie's shoulders.

That night, getting ready, the princess couldn't decide whether to carry the little dagger her parents had once given her for protection. She certainly had no intention of stabbing anyone. She tucked it in her belt beneath the cape.

At ten to midnight she slipped from her room and mounted the stairs to the tower. At the second turning she found Rosetta waiting, her long, constantly moving hair gleaming in the torchlight.

"If it's Riggeloff," Sylvie whispered, "what am I going to say? I can hardly threaten him."

"You'll think of something," Rosetta whispered back. "First, find out what he wants."

They floated the rest of the way up the stairs. Rosetta briefly poked her head out onto the ramparts, then ducked back in. "Nobody here," she whispered.

"Shh," said Sylvie, stepping past her into the open. The moon-silvered stones gleamed underfoot, while above her a banner luffed in an uncertain wind. Sylvie stood listening. What was that scraping sound in the corner where the walls met? She heard it again and recognized it as a laugh—a peculiar one, like a weasel coughing.

"Pingree?" she whispered.

A short, humanlike creature took a step forward, holding to one of the guide ropes. It was hard to make him out at first, silhouetted against the moony sky like a tin cutout. "The same," he said, and bowed.

She stared at him. "Impossible."

The jester moved farther away from the wall, and the moonlight slashed across his crooked features. "Perhaps. And yet you see him before you."

She gauged his puny arms. "I know you couldn't budge the tortoise, let alone hide him. And as for the fish—"

"Smelly creatures, fish, aren't they? How could you be friends with one?"

"As for the fish," she went on, "he'd swallow you in one gulp and still be hungry."

Pingree grinned. "And yet he did not."

"What have you done with him?" said Sylvie hotly.

"If I told you that, you'd know where to find him."

"All right," she said, "if you won't tell me what you've done, at least tell me *why*."

"Simple. Beautifully simple."

"It's not that old plan of taking over the kingdom, is it? You tried that once before."

"I was hoping you'd have forgotten that."

"It didn't work then, and it won't now."

"Calm yourself, dear," said the little man. "I have no desire to overthrow King Walther. Let the mildewy old fellow rule as long as he likes."

Sylvie well remembered Pingree's conspiracy with Prince Riggeloff years ago to take over the kingdom. They'd succeeded for a while, until she had managed to outwit them.

"No," mused Pingree, twirling his jester's cap around one finger and making the bell jingle, "I no longer have any ambitions, except . . ."

"Ah," said Sylvie. "Except."

"Except to do whatever you desire."

"I desire you to jump in the moat!"

"No, my dear, that is not quite it. You desire to go to your father and tell him how very much you long to marry me."

Sylvie, for one of the few times in her life, didn't know what to say.

"Lovely evening, isn't it, Princess?" he said. "So romantic."

"Stay away from me, lizard!"

"Come, let's take a stroll around the ramparts and

discuss our wedding plans." He slipped a pipelike arm around her waist.

She shook him off. "I'm warning you . . ."

"Naturally," he went on, "my status here will have to change. But it's a sacrifice I'm willing to make."

"What," Sylvie burst out, "are you blithering about?"

"Well, you *can't* marry a commoner, can you? Wouldn't be right." In the strange light his right eye glittered like a star. His left was dull and lifeless. You never knew where you stood, looking at Pingree.

"Don't you think I'm a little young for you?" she said. "You know, I'm twelve years old."

"Yes, but you've always been twelve years old. You're fictional. You'll be twelve forever."

"Anyway, why do you think I'd want to marry you?"

"Oh," he said, "the usual reasons: my wit, my gentle nature, the turn of my leg, and the fact that I have your animals."

Sylvie looked at him narrowly. "Is Riggeloff in this with you?"

"You cut me to the quick! Why would I need a ruffian like him to help me?"

"And if I don't marry you?"

"Bad choice."

"I doubt you can hurt my animals."

"Hurt them, no. But I can make them disappear. Forever." There was something hard in his voice that made Sylvie pause. She felt the need to be careful. "Suppose we do marry," she said.

"Yes, let's suppose that."

"You'd bring my animals back?"

"They would be attendants at our wedding," he declared. "We'd ride off on our honeymoon inside your invisible fish. We'd survey our kingdom from the back of the tortoise."

"*Our* kingdom?"

"Well, your father's kingdom, of course. But since I'd be his son-in-law . . ."

"I can imagine how he'd love that!"

"You would have to intercede for me. And you will."

"You seem quite sure of this."

"Oh, I am."

Sylvie reached in her robes and pulled out her dagger. Pingree's bright eye seemed to bulge. "What's that for?"

"To help us cut through those fancy words of yours."

"Now, Princess," he said, taking a step back. "You are not to hurt Pingree."

"Pingree is not to hurt my animals."

"I don't intend to."

"Pingree is not to blackmail the princess."

"I should mention," he said, quailing against the rampart, "that if anything happens to me, you'll never see those creatures again!"

"I wouldn't actually kill you, Pingree."

"Oh," he said.

"I'd just carve away small parts of you. Of course, those are the only kind of parts you have."

"Don't even jest about it!"

"Oh, I'm not. For one thing, I'm not a jester."

"Stop!"

"An ear here, a toe there. I'll have you whittled down to size in no time."

Pingree was shaking as he watched the blade come closer, glinting with intent. But then he had a thought, and the shaking diminished. Soon it stopped altogether. "All right," he said in his reedy voice, "go ahead."

Sylvie cocked her head to the side, as if she hadn't heard correctly.

"Go on," said the jester, drawing himself to his full height, such as it was.

"I will, then."

"Where do you want to start? Fingers? Nose? I've always thought my nose was a trifle long."

"What is this sudden show of bravery? You're a cowardly, lowly creature and always have been. It's the way your character is written."

Pingree smiled. "All true, I'm afraid," he said. "But you leave out one quality that the Author gave me in abundance."

"Ugliness?"

"Intelligence. I suddenly realized, in the midst of my cowardly squirming just now, that I had nothing to fear."

"Do you see this knife?"

"Yes, but I know how *your* character is written. There's not a touch of cruelty in it. You could no more cut off my nose than you would cut off your own."

Again Sylvie found herself without an answer.

"So let's put that away and stop pretending."

He was right. She might have a knife, but he had the advantage. In all her years as heroine of *The Great Good Thing*, she had never hurt anyone.

She looked up at the moon, that fake-looking, illustrator's moon, and sighed. "All right," she said at last. "What do you want me to do?"

chapter eight

I almost rushed out there a dozen times!" Rosetta exclaimed as she and Sylvie descended the dim staircase from the tower. "At first to tell that wretch what I thought of him. But then, toward the end . . ."

"I know, I know."

"I really thought you might . . . do something."

"He made me mad enough," Sylvie replied.

"I would have twisted his little arm till he *squeaked*!"

"He knew I wouldn't do that. He was right—I'm not written that way."

They reached the great hall, its tapestries and mounted shields glowing in the torchlight. "Well," said Rosetta, "I suppose I should get back home. What are you going to do?"

"Toss and turn. And then tomorrow I'll talk to my parents. Well, my father. Mother is still in bed recovering."

"Is she any better?"

"She complained about her food today."

"Was there something wrong with it?"

"Of course not. It just means she's starting to be her old self. If she's not unhappy, she's not happy."

"Well then, I'm glad. But, Sylvie, you can't marry Pingree!"

"I can't *not* marry him."

Rosetta's beautiful face wrinkled with distaste, and her flowing hair fled out behind her like a frightened cat. "We'll find a way," she said. "Meanwhile, put him off. Make preparations for the wedding, but don't complete them."

"That may work for a while."

"It will give us time. Those animals must be in the book somewhere."

Sylvie gave Rosetta a hug. "You are making me feel better," she said.

"Now go to bed and get a good night's tossing and turning."

"You too."

As it happened, both of them, exhausted by the emotions of the evening, slept like sacks of flour in a grain bin. Sylvie was wakened at midmorning by the glow of sunlight on her eyelids. She sat up, suddenly remembering everything. If only a Reader would come along, she thought, she could forget about all this and get involved in the familiar old story. But there hadn't been a Reader in ages—more sundials than she could count.

"Come *on*, Kara," Sylvie murmured as she slipped on her clothes. "Don't you want to read our story again?"

She brushed the worst of the tangles out of her hair and headed to the kitchen, where the cook cut her a slice of crusty bread and poured a mug of warm goat's milk. Sylvie liked eating here, with the servants chattering and kittens tumbling over one another and the sun pouring in the window. So much friendlier than the dim dining hall where her parents took their meals. But she couldn't stay here avoiding what she had to do. She twisted off a piece of bread for later, then climbed the stairs. Outside the king's chamber she took a deep breath.

King Walther's reaction to her news was surprisingly mild. "Can't we just wring the jester's neck?" he asked reasonably.

"I can't," she said. "And I don't think I could let you do it either."

"I could do it without telling you."

"You just did. No, I'm afraid I have to deal with this in my own way."

"At all costs we must keep it from your mother. The queen is in too delicate a state."

"How can we do that?"

"I don't know, but her recovery depends on it. She must be ceaselessly well deceived."

"That's another thing I'm not made for—lying."

"Then we must keep *you* away from her."

"With a wedding to plan?"

He sighed in exasperation. "You think of something! You're the heroine."

"I'm trying!"

"Where is your friend, the one with the eyes?"

"Laurel?"

"That's it. She always has good ideas."

"I'm looking for her."

"Well, find her. This has got me all fuddled."

He looked more than fuddled. He looked helpless. "Don't worry, Father," said Sylvie, going to him and stroking his kingly hair. "We'll find a way."

He looked at her with a confusion of hope. "Thank you, daughter."

Sylvie's mind was in turmoil as she left. Where was Laurel when she needed her? For now Sylvie had to depend on herself. She climbed the cliff over the Mere and whistled for the blind owl. He happened to be nearby, preening his feathers, and came quickly. "Well, little one," she murmured as he yanked her into the air, "let's take another look around."

They circled and recircled the kingdom. Nothing. Unless the tortoise was at the back of a cave, she mused, or the fish was at the bottom of the Mere, the animals were no longer in the book. In these days of light gravity, fewer and fewer things were at the bottom of the Mere. Some even floated above it.

She had the owl drop her off at Rosetta's hut, and that afternoon the two young women set out together, pushing off from one rock and gliding side by side to the next. There were several caverns they knew about. One of them had bats—thousands sleeping upside down in rows—but none held invisible fish or ten-foot tortoises.

Resting beneath an overhanging rock, Sylvie and Rosetta looked out over the valley. "Wait," Sylvie said, standing up. "Humped Mountain! The inside is full of hollows."

"We've looked everywhere else."

Getting inside the mountain would not be easy. The only entrance Sylvie had ever used was deep in the Mere, accessible by way of the invisible fish.

"What about the waterfall?" Rosetta said, pointing.

"Poor old waterfall," said Sylvie.

Brilliant in sunlight, the water gushed from the bald rock near the top of the mountain, but lacking gravity, it bent outward like long hair in the wind.

"I mean," said Rosetta, "*behind* the waterfall."

"You're right." Sylvie surveyed the tumult of water blurting from the mountain. "There is an opening, if you can get to it."

"Couldn't we just fly over?"

"Too far," said Sylvie. "No matter how hard we pushed off, we'd slow down before we got there. We'd be hanging in the air."

"How about the owl?"

"He could carry me. I'm not sure he trusts anyone else."

Rosetta gave a pretty frown.

"That's all right," Sylvie said. "I'll go by myself."

"Not a good idea."

Sylvie wasn't listening. She climbed on top of the overhanging rock and gave a piercing whistle. She waited, then let out another. On the third a speck appeared over the mountain's shoulder. It was the owl.

"Thank you!" she said as the owl's talons curled through her harness straps. "Could you take me to the waterfall, please?"

The great bird lurched into the air and wheeled about underneath the falls. The water quaked and sloshed.

"Under the edge!" Sylvie called out. "Underneath!" By pointing and shouting, Sylvie was finally able to get the bird to understand. It tilted away, then swooped beneath the water and into the cave.

A network of caves, really. This was the topmost one, the chamber where the Keeper of the Cave of Diamonds came to sleep. Just now it was empty, the waterfall filtering the light to a shimmering kaleidoscope against the rocks. Along with the reds and blues, points of white light glistened. Diamonds. The mountain was studded with them.

The owl slipped its talons from the harness and hurtled away, leaving Sylvie to explore the dripping tunnels, some with torches bracketed to the walls, others with no light at all. Down she wound into the recesses of the mountain. Once she hit her head on a stalactite; another time she stopped just before the path broke away into an abyss.

She called out in a low voice, "Fish! Fish!" and sometimes, "Tortoise, are you there?" Her words echoed back like a mocking spirit.

Soon she came to a level space where the path broadened out. It was a work area of some kind, to judge by the wood shavings that littered the ground. What was the Keeper making?

Sylvie continued on till the path narrowed to nothing; then she turned and started back up. Her foot kicked against some dry leaves.

Leaves? she thought. *In a cave?*

She picked up several. Eucalyptus leaves, mangled and torn.

The tortoise! She realized it hadn't been here recently. The leaves were dusty and curled like claws. Still, she called out, her voice bouncing in the darkness.

The path rose steeply, and she had to concentrate on not missing her footing. She glanced ahead. *Hadn't noticed that boulder up there,* she thought, then realized with a jolt that it was not a boulder, but a living creature, malevolent and humped with muscle, blocking the path.

"Who's in my cave?" The voice was as harsh as iron and octaves deep. Princess Sylvie recognized it instantly. After all, she had to deal with the same adversary every time a Reader came to this part of the story.

Sylvie hated this part of the story.

"I—I," she began. "I didn't mean to intrude."

"Get out!"

Sylvie controlled her panic by taking a long deep breath, then another, as Rosetta had taught her to do in times of stress. *"Just take deep abdominal breaths,"* Rosetta had said. Unfortunately, the only word Sylvie could think of now was *abominable.*

"Excuse me, sir," she said, when her heart had slowed a bit. "I have to ask you something."

"You come to torment me when we don't even have a *Reader?*" he roared.

"Yes, sir."

"Leave!" The savage old man turned and, with

remarkable agility, clambered up a rock that hung over the path.

"Stop!" she called out. "I want to know what you've done with my tortoise!"

He looked around at her. "What would I do with your tortoise? He's too tough to eat."

"He was here. Right where I'm standing." Sylvie paused. Angry as she was, it made no sense to threaten someone twice her size and ten times her strength. "Don't you realize," she said quietly, "we need those animals for our story?"

"Don't talk to me. I *hate* the story!"

"You do?"

"What do you think? That I *like* turning into that weak-brained Godric?"

"I know you and Prince Godric have had your differences . . ."

He spat. A great green gob landed on the edge of a rock and dripped, not down, but outward.

She tilted her head to get a better look at him. "Is that," she said, "why you're helping the jester? Because you don't like the story?"

"The jester? I *hate* the jester!"

"You hate everyone. But you're helping him. Why?"

His lopsided head seemed to hum with thought. "Smart, en't you?"

"Smart enough," she answered, "to know that Pingree's a weakling. He could never handle the tortoise by himself. How'd you get him in here?"

"En't telling."

"Did he give you much of a fight?"

His bulgy eye narrowed. "You're trying to trick me, en't you?"

Sylvie smiled and ducked her head. "You caught me."

"Ha!" He swung himself on top of a rock and sat, his misshapen legs sticking out of his tattered trousers. "I'm not so dumb as I look."

Sylvie felt a new excitement. She was actually having a *conversation* with this monstrous man. Usually their relationship involved his screaming and her standing her ground. "Oh, you don't look dumb at all," she said soothingly.

"Don't lie! I know what I look like. The Author put in plenty of descriptions."

"Oh, I'm sure she didn't mean—"

"I'm the stupid old monster of the mountain. I'm the one you feel sorry for at the end of the story."

"I don't feel sorry for you," she said. "You scare me too much."

"Good!"

"So," she said, looking as humble as possible, "how did you manage it? I can't believe that even you would be that strong."

He swung his furry shins back and forth. "Don't need to be strong."

"You don't?"

"You're forgetting. Things don't weigh much these days."

"But still, just the size . . ."

"Uh-uh! Trying to trick me again!"

Sylvie shook her head. "You're too smart for me."

Something weirdly like a smile came over his face, giving him a ghastly expression. No one, certainly, had called him smart before. "And don't forget your precious fish," he added with a smug look.

"What do you mean?"

"When he's out of the water, he dries up."

"Of course! And you just rolled him up?"

"En't saying."

"Do you have him stashed away somewhere?"

His eyes were alight with self-satisfaction. It didn't make him any more attractive.

"Come on," Sylvie coaxed.

"Uh-uh!" the Keeper warned.

"But I've looked everywhere else!"

"Bet you have."

Sylvie had only so much patience, even with creatures as fearsome as this. "You give me back my animals!" she burst out.

"Aw," he said, "the widdle pwincess is unhappy."

"Stop that!"

"The pwetty little hewoine, who gets to do all the gweat good things. What a shame!"

"Stop it, you horrible creature!"

"Yes, horrible! *Now* you're honest! But you've got no idea what suffering's about." As he thrust his face forward the gleam of torchlight lit up the wound on his forehead. It's a wound that never heals until the end of the story, when Princess Sylvie, overcome by pity, kisses it, breaking the spell.

"Author's got a lot to answer for, is what I think," he said bitterly. "What did it cost her to scribble a few lines about the old Keeper of the Cave?" He spat in the darkness. "Let's see, we'll make him ugly, yes, *horrible* ugly. And then we'll have him be in pain every minute. That's rich, en't it? And give him a dripping wound on his head. Then we'll coop him up inside Humped Mountain, a mountain as humped as himself."

"I'm sorry."

"I don't want your sorrow, missy."

"What do you want?"

"I want the story to be over—for good!"

"And you think the jester can help you?"

"When he gets power, he'll change the story and let me out of here."

A sudden tremor ran through the cave, sending a rivulet of stones trickling past Sylvie's feet. From somewhere outside came a commotion of voices.

"What's *that*?" said the Keeper, wheeling around.

Sylvie started scrambling toward the upper cave, where the waterfall was. "Maybe we're getting a Reader."

"No!" groaned the Keeper. "Keep 'im away!"

Sylvie raced up to the Keeper's sleeping cave, where the wall of stone opened to the tumult of the falls. She could make out blurry outlines of dials and gauges overhead but saw no one. No time to summon the owl, she realized. Shutting her eyes tight and gulping a breath, she dove straight through the cascade.

The water was frigid, and she came out swimming

hard as the strange, suspended watercourse curved away from the mountainside. She grabbed another breath and dove down until she broke through the bottom of the water. Dangling in midair, she glanced at the liquid ceiling, then down at the glittering Mere. It would have been a dizzy and dangerous fall, but with so little gravity, Sylvie merely hovered like a gull till she remembered Rosetta's instructions on how to make herself heavy. It took several long minutes, but finally she entered the Mere as gently as if she were stepping into a bath.

She heard shouts and crashes overhead. It had been months since she'd heard those voices, but she knew them right away.

"Hey!" It was Matt's voice, shouting. "Cut it out!"

"I'll take that, if you don't mind." Wink's voice, sounding strained.

The kingdom began shaking back and forth, creating a slosh of water in the Mere. One of the waves curled over Sylvie's head, and she came up sputtering.

"Let go!" Kara cried. "Leave my book alone!"

"Listen to me, Wink!" came Matt's voice. "We're almost home. Don't blow it!"

"You mean, don't blow it for *you*!"

"Wink, Wink!" said Matt. "Listen. Have you taken your meds?"

"Medicine? Why?"

"You need to take them *now*."

"You know they slow me down."

"That's what we need. Slow and steady."

"You want to mess up my performance even more, don't you?"

Sylvie stared up but could see very little through the film of water.

"Wink!" cried Kara. "Let go! You're going to tear the book!"

"Good!"

There was a horrible ripping sound, and most of a page about the Keeper of the Cave tore away.

"Now look!" Kara sounded furious.

"You want it back?"

Sylvie then heard a truly frightening sound: paper being crumpled into a ball.

"Here," Wink shouted. "Catch!"

"No!"

The waters parted in time for Sylvie to see Kara flash by in front of the open book and disappear.

"*Heartland*, this is Mission Control."

"Wink!" cried Matt. "Listen to me! We need you for reentry! If we miss it, we die! Can you understand that? Do you want us to die?"

"*Now* you need me! You sent me in to PAM most of yesterday."

"You needed to be monitored for new meds!"

"Oh, the old ones didn't mess me up enough?"

"*Heartland*, this is Houston. Do you read?"

"Roger, Houston, we read you," said Matt's voice.

"I'm *through* with your damn meds!" Wink gave the book a cuff that sent it spinning. Sylvie and the others held on as best they could as the book caromed around the cabin. The Mere and the waterfall leaped and curled.

"Ready to initiate reentry procedure," came the voice over the speaker.

"Ready to initiate," confirmed Matt. "Wink, get over here and sit down!"

"I don't know, Commander. I wouldn't want to screw things up."

"Everything secured, *Heartland*? You don't want things flying around when gravity kicks in."

"Check, Houston," said Matt.

"We've got a book flying around right now," cried Wink, his voice slightly hysterical. "Look at 'er go!"

"*Heartland*, can you tell us what's happening up there?"

"We seem to be having a little disagreement here, Houston," Matt said.

Kara's angry voice rang out: "Wink refuses to do his job!"

"Oh, buzz off, Kara!" shouted Wink. Through the sloshing water, Sylvie caught a glimpse of his outstretched hands shoving her violently. There was a metallic crash, immediately followed by a lurch that raised the Mere right out of its banks. A high wave rolled Sylvie under for several frightening seconds.

Desperate, she fought her way up, breaking the surface and coughing for air in time to hear the voice on the loudspeaker calling, "*Heartland*, you are accelerating! Repeat: You are accelerating!"

"Copy, Houston," came Matt's voice. He was breathing hard.

"Reduce speed immediately!"

"Roger, Houston. We're—"

"Reduce at once or you'll bounce off Earth's atmosphere like a stone skipping off a pond! Do you copy?"

"We have a problem, Houston."

"*Heartland*, can you reduce speed or not?"

"The controls aren't responding! When Kara was thrown against them—"

There was sudden silence, lasting several endless seconds. The voice of Mission Control came on again. "*Heartland*, do you read? Come in, *Heartland*."

After a long pause Matt's voice answered. He sounded weary. "This is *Heartland*."

"*Heartland*, this is Houston. It's too late. Do you read? *It's too late. You've missed reentry.*"

PART THREE

time

chapter nine

No one bothered closing the book. It came to rest near the ceiling and just hung there, ignored and unread, its pages waving gently as the crew members rushed back and forth making adjustments that they seemed to know were useless. Matt fixed the acceleration (it proved a minor glitch), but that didn't make anyone happier. Suddenly nothing seemed to matter very much. Eventually, the activity slackened off; and the messages from Houston, so frequent and urgent at first, almost ceased. Now and then one of the astronauts came by, looking preoccupied.

Fangl listened carefully, trying to make sense of the talk about trajectories. As he interpreted it for Sylvie, by skipping off the atmosphere, the ship was being flung out in an enormous ellipse, as if by a slingshot. The force would carry them as far into space as they had gone before, all the way to Jupiter, before rounding the turn and heading back. If the trip took as long as before, it would be four years before the crew had another shot at entering Earth's atmosphere. Of course, that was possible only at certain times, at a certain angle, and at a specific speed. The *Heartland*'s air supply would have given out long before that. The ship would be a supersonic coffin hurtling through space until, some centuries in the future, it passed close enough to a planet to enter its orbit, and then it would either become a tiny moon or crash into the planet's surface.

"Well, for now they've got food," Fangl murmured as he peered out from the half-open pages.

"How do you know?" Sylvie said.

"Ever since Kara repaired the diodes, most of the plants have been growing well. The crew might get tired of wheatgrass and Swiss chard, but they shouldn't starve. If it came to it, they could even eat their experimental animals."

Sylvie wrinked up her face. "The mice?"

"Protein is protein."

"Of course," said Laurel, breaking in, "food doesn't mean very much if you can't breathe. Lucky for us," she said, "we don't eat Reader food or breathe Reader air."

"That won't save us if the ship is destroyed," Fangl said.

"What can we do?" said Sylvie.

Laurel puffed out a sigh. "I don't know. Remember, we don't exist out there."

"I never understood that," said Sylvie. "We're real. They're real."

"But we're in different realities."

"Then why do we feel the cold?"

"Because the book gets cold, and we live in the book."

"So there are crossovers," said Sylvie. "And it's not only that we feel the same temperature."

Laurel looked at her. "What do you mean?"

"Sometimes our realities cross. When Kara's reading and she's concentrating hard, I feel . . ." Sylvie held open her hands. "It's like we're doing it together."

"Yes," Laurel said quietly. "The barrier gets very thin."

The friends grew thoughtful.

"I like her so much," Sylvie said after a while.

"Me too."

"I don't want her to die."

The lights dimmed in the cabin. Matt's voice could be heard over the intercom ordering the powering down of electrical systems. The rocket's engine was also shut off. There was no point using up fuel. In fact, except for course corrections, there'd be no need for fuel during the next four years.

Fangl cleared his throat. "So if I understand it, the problem now is air."

Laurel nodded. "They have food enough. And the water is all recycled."

"*All* of it?" said Sylvie.

"Almost all," Fangl agreed. "It's purified and used again."

"Even . . . ?"

"Even urine is recycled, yes, if that's what you mean, after it's been run through the purification system," Fangl said.

Sylvie gave a little shiver. "I'm glad we drink imaginary water."

"Much the best kind. But about the air . . ." He bit his underlip and closed his eyes. "There has *got* to be a way."

"What about—?" Sylvie began. "No, you said they have enough water."

"What, Princess?" Fangl said.

"No, I was just thinking about all that ice they loaded, when we were on that moon. It must be melted now."

"Yes! Of course!"

"But you can't breathe water," said Sylvie.

"No, you can't, Princess, quite right, absolutely right. My dear, I think you've just solved it!"

"I don't understand."

"Now if only we could communicate with *them*. It wouldn't take much, just a suggestion. They're smart enough to figure out the rest."

"The rest of *what*?" cried Sylvie. "Fangl, you make me crazy!"

"Princess, do you think you could get inside of Kara's mind? I know you've done it with Readers in the past."

"Well," she said doubtfully, "if we could get her to dream about the story, then I could hop over the margin and into her dreams. But with all the things on her mind just now . . ."

"True, true."

"I'm afraid we'll just have to wait and hope."

"I don't know how much time we have."

They were interrupted just then by a young messenger, a bouncing fellow whose skinny legs were accentuated by purple tights. He bowed expertly. "The king," he announced, "would like to see all three of you in the small council chamber."

"Even me?" said Fangl, who was often left out of high-level meetings.

"His Majesty particularly mentioned you, Master Fangl."

Sylvie and Laurel shot each other a look as they headed down the stone corridor behind the energetic servant. They were escorted into a low-ceilinged room where King Walther and three of his most trusted councillors were seated around a table. He thanked everyone for coming and then said what they all knew, that the voyage had run into trouble and that the kingdom was again in terrible danger. He asked for suggestions.

His Chief Councillor, a large, florid-faced man in his middle years, merely shook his head.

After a silence the oldest councillor, a wizened fellow whose forehead protruded over his nose, coughed in disgust. "With respect, I don't believe a word of it."

"A word of what, Warburton?" said the king.

"Missing Earth. How can you miss Earth?"

"I don't follow you," said the king.

"It would be like falling down and missing the ground. What these Readers are saying, simply, is that they *miss* Earth. They miss the things of Earth. Daisies and houses, that sort of thing. Who could blame them?"

"Yes, but—"

"Are we in danger?" Warburton went on. "Yes. We've been in danger ever since this misbegotten voyage began.

You all felt the wave of cold that nearly froze us to our bones some months ago. We're in perpetual danger! But in no more danger than we were." The old man fell into a coughing fit, hawking up phlegm into a lace handkerchief and waving his arm to signify he was finished talking.

"I see, yes. Anyone else?" King Walther cast his eyes around.

The girl with the dark blue eyes gave him a nod.

"Laurel?"

"I believe, Your Majesty, that Mr. Fangl has a thought."

The king turned to the geometer.

"My thoughts, Your Majesty," said Fangl, "are not formed. I haven't done the math on them. But I have an idea that might prolong the lives of our friends aboard the spaceship."

"That would certainly help."

"The problem is how to communicate with them. Would you give me permission to conduct an experiment?"

"What sort of experiment?"

"Changing the order of some of the words in Chapter One."

"Must you?"

"I see no other way, Your Highness."

"Well, if you must, you must."

Fangl bowed as low as his old body would permit.

"What are you going to do, Fangl?" hissed Sylvie when they were out in the corridor.

"I'm thinking," he said, "if we can somehow get a message to Kara, it might—"

"Can I help?" she said.

"Meet me in the first chapter. You too, Miss Laurel, if you're willing."

"Of course," she replied.

An eighth of a sundial later they had done what they could. It hadn't been easy prying out letters that had been embedded in the page since the book was published. And then they had to find places to put the extra letters they had displaced. Several sentences now made no sense whatever, but that couldn't be helped. They would put everything back later, once they'd gotten their message across.

If they got it across. For the longest time Kara didn't come near the book, and she was the only one who had ever been interested in it. A day went by—or a whole sundial, as the book's characters thought of it. Then another day. The astronauts weren't moving about the ship as much as they had before, and when they did come by, Sylvie could hear their breathing. It sounded as though they were climbing a steep hill.

"The air," she whispered to Fangl. "It's beginning to run out."

"You're right, Princess."

Some hours later Kara's face appeared. She looked pale. Picking the book up, she carried it to a workstation and laid it open at the place where Wink had torn a page out. Her hands trembling, Kara unwadded a ball of paper and placed it, wrinkled as it was, where it belonged. She then took a strip of tape and reattached the page. It wasn't a perfect job; her hands were shaking too much. But if you hopped over some misaligned words, you could get the gist.

She stared at the page, a description of the caverns in Humped Mountain. A large warm tear fell onto the second paragraph, waking a ledge of sleeping bats.

"Good-bye, dear book." Kara's voice was a rasping whisper.

Sylvie looked up from the page and shouted, "Read it! Read the story!"

Kara carried the book with her around the cabin, moving with effort. Then she headed to the sleeping compartment, where she lay down and slung her arm over her eyes.

"Read it, Kara! Start at the beginning!"

The compartment was dim, but a vague diffusion of light came through the window.

Finally Kara sat up on her elbow, opened the book, and leafed slowly past the title and copyright pages.

"Yes!" Sylvie shouted, jumping in the air.

An orange bird flew from the nostril of a gargoyle. *"Rawwwk!* Reader! Reader!"

"We know! We know!" cried Sylvie.

From the moat, a frog with the voice of a tuba warned: "Oooopen! Booook open!"

Tripping over their gowns, six ladies-in-waiting fussed into the throne room, where the first scene always began.

"Father," cried Sylvie, "I cannot marry Prince Riggeloff!"

The king had not said his lines in months, and his performance showed it. "Not, um, marry Riggeloff?" He cleared his throat. "For heaven's sake, child, he is, um, handsome, rich—"

"**breathe moon water!**" cried Sylvie. "**ind ve cninud icss Syli I a ae f is.**"

"He has everything," the king said, blinking.

"**evaPoraKe!**" Sylvie shouted. "**quliis S hve I.**"

"That, uh, may be," stammered the king, flummoxed by his daughter's response, "but you still don't have a husband."

"What?" Kara stopped to read the last few lines again. "evaPoraKe?" she murmured. "quliis S hve I? What is this, Latin?"

She shook the book as if the words would fall back into their accustomed places. They stayed where they were. "evaPoraKe," she whispered. "I'm hallucinating. The lack of air is getting to me."

She closed the book.

Sylvie and Laurel looked at each other. Fangl trotted in from the next page. "What happened?" he said. "Did she read it?"

"She read it," said Laurel. "She just didn't believe it."

"She doesn't have to believe it!" Fangl stamped his narrow foot. "She just has to do it!"

"Not believing is not seeing," Laurel replied.

Fangl sat down on a tuffet and held his head in his hands.

Sylvie laid her hand on his shoulder. "You did what you could."

He shook his head without looking at her.

Suddenly the book flew open. The pages rattled past—title, copyright, acknowledgments, contents— and there was Kara, a little wild-eyed, looking down into Chapter One.

"Matt!" she called. "Come here!"

chapter ten

For God's sake, can't you hurry it up?" came a sharp voice from somewhere.

"Look, Wink, you did an amazing job rigging this thing up," came Kara's voice, "but we can't just start putting the water through it before we know what we've got."

"It's not like we're *drinking* it," he cut in. "Whatever microbes or other junk is in there will separate out in the evaporation process."

"We *hope*. But you know what happened to the mice when I gave them some of the water."

"Maybe it was too concentrated. Anyway, this will be air, not water."

"I'm afraid Wink is right," came Matt's deeper voice. "We've got less than six hours of oxygen left. I don't see that we have a choice."

"I know, I know." Kara's voice sounded strained. "Just give me . . ."

"How long?" said Matt.

"An hour?"

"I need air now!" Wink shrilled.

"Don't you think *I* do?" she shot back. "Look, we know the water contains biomorphing microbes. That's why we were sent to bring back so much of it."

"Really?" Wink's voice was harsh. "I thought we went all that way to bury some baseball cards in the ice."

"To be fair," said Matt, "they had to tell people something. There'd be riots in the streets if they'd told them the truth."

Kara's face could be seen through the half-open pages. "Guys, I just want to test the air we're producing before we put it into our lungs. Is that asking too much?"

"I can give you half an hour," said Matt.

Kara gave a heavy sigh. Then she had to breathe in deeply to make up for it.

"Don't dawdle, kid," said Wink, climbing down the hatch.

"Hey," she said in a lowered voice.

Matt looked at her.

"He seems better today."

"You can tell when he's taking his meds, can't you?" Matt murmured.

"Wish he'd been doing that the other day," she said.

"No kidding," he said.

"We'd be home by now, and I'd be taking a real, honest-to-goodness shower."

"I'd be making myself a big peanut-butter-and-jelly sandwich on fresh rye bread."

"We're out of peanut butter?"

"We're out of most things. Well, I'm going to pretend to be busy for a while. See you."

"Right."

Sylvie leaned over and whispered to Fangl. "Do you know what they meant by—what was it? Morphing?"

"Biomorphing? Haven't the slightest idea."

"I thought you knew everything."

He smiled gently.

Through the half-open pages, they glimpsed Kara as she checked gauges and went from the microscope to the improvised vapor machine. Sometimes she had to stop and catch her breath, hunching over her work space and taking in gulps of thinning air.

"How about it?" Wink was back and looking over her shoulder.

"It hasn't been thirty minutes."

"It's been twenty-two. You must have some results. Or were you just going to tell *him*?"

"That's nutty."

"Is it?" He turned away. Looking up from the page, Sylvie thought she could see the jealousy working at him.

"Wink, please," Kara said.

"'Wink, *please*!' It would be just like you. 'Why give our precious air to Wink, that hopeless screwup?'"

"Stop it now! You can stop this, Wink."

"And what a convenient way to get rid of me!"

"Do you want to hear the results or not?"

He was breathing hard but trying to control it. He closed his eyes and nodded.

"I don't have anything definitive. There may be some residue in the vapor. I need to do more tests."

"Which we don't have time for."

"That's right."

"How long would they take?"

"Hours."

"So?"

She looked at him and nodded. "Start filling the air tanks."

"Umph oo gomph?" Rosetta paused, pins in her mouth, as she held the hem of Sylvie's bridal gown. In the low gravity the satin kept ballooning out.

"Say again?"

Rosetta stuck the pins into a pincushion that was tied to a chair leg that was nailed to the floor. Sylvie stood above her on a platform. "I said, aren't you going? You know. To Pingree's ceremony."

"Oh, please, Rose!"

"It's not every day a jester is elevated to a prince."

"It's one day too many."

"Still, if he's going to be your husband . . ." Rosetta was squinting at the hemline. It was hard to measure when it kept floating up.

"Rosetta," said Sylvie, "are you purposely trying to upset me?"

The pins were in Rosetta's mouth again. "Forry."

The royal seamstress, a round-faced woman with escaping wisps of white hair, hovered about nervously, along with her assistant. "Can't I help?" she said. "I'm worried your friend is going to hurt herself with those pins."

"Thank you, Mistress Wimble," said Sylvie, "but I'm afraid you're too good at this. You'd have the dress done in a day, and it would be perfect."

"Thank you, Your Highness."

"That's why you won't do."

"I see."

"Anyway, Rosetta needs the practice. She's never made anything like this before."

Wimble almost stuttered. "Practice on a wedding gown?"

"One must start somewhere."

"Iv thif long enough?" said Rosetta.

Sylvie studied herself in the tall looking glass. "It's good. It's perfect. Change it."

Rosetta looked up at her.

"So we can alter it again tomorrow," Sylvie explained. "We don't want to be ready too soon. Not that it matters."

Rosetta finished putting in the last of the pins. "What doesn't matter?"

"Well, the way things are going, either I marry Pingree and we all crash into a planet, or I *don't* marry Pingree and we crash into a planet."

"Oh!" cried Wimble.

"Cheery of you," Rosetta said.

"Assuming we get close to a planet."

"Hey. Enough."

"Or we may just float on forever."

"All right," Rosetta said, standing up, "Come with me. We're getting out of here."

"Where are we going?"

"The cook will fix us a basket. We're going on a picnic."

"Sounds nice."

"Better than having you turn sour on me."

Sylvie stepped out of the half-finished dress and hopped from the platform. She noticed that the dress remained suspended in air. "Good-bye, Mistress Wimble," she said, nodding to the seamstress. "We'll continue tomorrow."

She skimmed out the door, holding on to the guide ropes as she and Rosetta hurried to the kitchen. Minutes later they were passing under the portcullis, a basket of food on Sylvie's arm.

Much as they would have liked to ignore the impending marriage, it was impossible not to discuss it.

"He's a strange one, that Pingree," Rosetta said.

"He is. Most suitors would be sending love notes," said Sylvie. "He sends me warnings. 'Don't delay this wedding anymore!'"

The Mere of Remind glinted up ahead, its wavelets tipped in red, blue, and orange. Above, the waterfall continued not to fall.

"I'll be happy when we have gravity again," said Rosetta. "Do you really think we might fly on forever?"

"You heard them."

"At least they've got air. What is it? Something else is bothering you."

The friends sat on a twist of driftwood. "It's just that nothing we do seems to matter," Sylvie said after a bit. "When we have Readers, we run around acting out our little story. When we *don't* have Readers, well, look at Pingree. He's always figuring how to look important."

"He's a ridiculous creature," said Rosetta firmly.

"We're all ridiculous creatures. Look up, Rosetta. The spaceship is doomed, and here we are planning a wedding."

"That doesn't sound like you, Sylvie. You never say something's doomed. You say, 'How can I fix it?'"

"Well, how can we?"

"I don't know, but you're the one always telling me that things will turn out well at the end of the story."

"I suppose."

"Have a sandwich."

Sylvie sank her teeth into a roast boar and cucumber sandwich garnished with dill weed. "I'm mainly worried about my animals."

"I know you are."

"What if we go through this whole wedding and he doesn't give them back?"

"You mean you don't trust Prince Pingree?"

"Don't call him that."

"You'd better get used to it."

"Poor Father." She puffed out a sigh. "Mother's not ecstatic either. We had to tell her, now that she's almost better."

Rosetta looked up at the yellow and blue cliffs. As she watched, the wind shifted and the stones turned red as sunlight struck the waterfall from a new angle. "At least you don't have grown men beating each other unconscious over you."

"Speaking of which . . ."

A man on a horse of many colors was trotting toward them along the shore—or just above the shore, the horse's hooves pawing the air as often as the ground. It was the lovesick thief, Thomas, and he had a flower in his teeth, which he intended to give to Rosetta, if he could keep from floating past her.

Sylvie couldn't help giggling as she watched his attempts to dismount.

"Thank you, Thomas," Rosetta said, accepting the red, then yellow, then blue rose. "It's unusual to see you without Prince Godric nipping at your heels."

"I left him tangled in a gore bush, Miss Stein."

Rosetta shook her head. "Thomas, you two have got to stop fighting. Do you think it makes me admire you?"

"I hadn't thought about it that way."

"You should. I'm fed up with you both."

He hung his head. "Forgive me."

"No," she answered. "Forgive *him*."

"How can I?"

Sylvie leaned forward. "Rosetta," she said, "I have a thought. Instead of fighting, why don't they *do* something?"

"But," said Thomas, overhearing, "don't I write her poems? Don't I bring her presents?"

"Not what I mean," Sylvie said.

Rosetta was looking at her with interest. "You mean something *important*?"

"That's right. Whoever hopes to win the hand of Miss Stein must accomplish a great good thing."

"Yes!" Rosetta cried. "But what would it be? You've cornered the market on great good things."

"I have an idea about that, too." She whispered to her friend, who nodded vigorously.

Rosetta cleared her throat. "First, let's understand, I'm not sure I'd marry either one of you. But whoever *hopes* to marry me . . ." She paused.

"What? I'll do anything."

". . . must first rescue Sylvie's animals!"

"The tortoise, you mean?" said Thomas. "And that fish nobody can see?"

"Correct. And whoever fights with the other contestant will automatically be disqualified."

"Disqualified!" murmured Thomas. "But—"

"But what?"

"Whenever I see Godric—"

"See him differently, Thomas, or don't expect to see me again. Now go back and help the prince out of the briar patch or wherever you left him and send him to me."

He ducked his head in a short bow. He kept lingering.

"*Now*, Thomas."

He nodded and turned back the way he'd come, walking beside his nearly airborne horse.

"Do you think it'll work?" Rosetta whispered.

"Even if it doesn't, it keeps them out of your hair," said Sylvie. "And if they succeed . . ."

"It saves you from Pingree!"

Sadness flitted across Sylvie's face. "I hope they're all right."

"Oh, they're fine, except for a few lumps on the head."

"I mean the tortoise and my beautiful invisible fish. I hope they're being taken care of. Maybe I'll take another look around the forest." Sylvie stood up, threw her head back, and sent forth a loud whistle across the Mere.

No response.

She tried again, even louder. "Poor owl," she said. "It's so hard for him. He's probably struggling to get over the mountain."

She whistled again.

"Oh no!" she whispered. Her heart was beating fast. "Not the owl, too!"

The owl was gone.

chapter eleven

It had been a long time since *The Great Good Thing* was opened. In the rush of events on the spaceship the book had been misplaced or tucked in a cubby and forgotten. Suddenly, with no warning from birds or bullfrogs, the book snapped open and Kara's face peered in.

At least it looked like Kara's face. It was rounder somehow, less defined, and her voice when she spoke was different too. For one thing, she giggled.

"Oh, Matt!" she called out. "It's that story! It's been here all the time."

"Good going," came a voice from somewhere. "Now if you could find us some rocket fuel and maybe a secondary source of electricity . . ."

"You're not funny."

Matt's face, minus the comfortable fatherly lines, appeared above the page. "I never got around to reading this. Is it any good?"

"Not for you."

"Why not? You don't think I have the imagination for it?"

She laughed her three-pronged laugh. "What would you do with imagination? It would only get in your way."

"So young and yet so cruel."

She looked at him sideways. "Have you been doing something different lately?"

"What do you mean?"

"You look more rested or something."

"I don't know about that, but I do feel"—he gave the neck of his T-shirt a pull—"very good."

"Me too."

"You *look* good."

"A compliment from the commander?"

"I mean, you look different. Have you done something with your hair?"

"New scrunchy."

"Must be it."

Sylvie was shamelessly looking up. A lot of characters were.

Matt looked around to be sure they were not overheard. "Do you know that little bald spot you guys have been ribbing me about?"

"Not so little."

"Well, take a look." He bent his head forward.

Kara frowned. "Where is it?"

"It's gone! I thought I was crazy."

"Wink looks different too, don't you think? Has he been into the chocolate supply?"

"Why?"

"His face is all broken out."

"Hadn't noticed."

"It's like he's a teenager."

"Well, he *is* the youngest."

She smirked. "Think that accounts for the mood swings?"

"I wish."

They looked at each other in silence. Finally Matt cleared his throat. "So can I borrow this or what?"

"Go ahead. But if you come back believing in invisible fish, don't blame me."

The book closed. Probably Matt intended to read it right away, but he didn't get to it for a long time. Meanwhile, Sylvie had to deal with Pingree.

But Pingree was refusing to be dealt with. He would not accept postponing the wedding any longer. "The game is over, Princess. I win, three animals to nothing."

"You're a cruel, horrible person."

"That is as it may be. I give you a dozen sundials."

"But I haven't even—"

"*Twelve sundials.* After that I start erasing the animals."

Sylvie couldn't answer, torn as she was between fury and terror. She was tempted to tell her father to use whatever force was necessary to make the jester return the animals. Finally she couldn't. Anyway, they had to be careful. The animals were not only Sylvie's dear creatures; they were also part of the plot. If they didn't return, the story would not make sense.

More search parties were sent out, using topographical maps to identify out-of-the-way nooks and valleys. "Don't forget," Sylvie cautioned. "The fish may not look like a fish. When it's out of the water, it can be rolled up like a parchment scroll. For all we know, it could be in the royal archives, filed under 'Ichthyology.'"

Pingree was enjoying the commotion. He could often be seen in his full princely getup standing on the parapet. Sylvie wanted to slap him. Instead, she took long walks, often with Laurel or Rosetta. "We've searched the caves, dredged the Mere, and looked between every set of parentheses. What else can we do?"

Laurel gave her a look. "We can try to figure out what's going on in Pingree's mind."

"Not a pretty place," Sylvie said.

"No, and not as simple as you might think. I know a bit about the way his mind works, and he still surprises me."

"Well, he couldn't do it by himself. Somehow he got the Keeper of the Cave to go along."

"I can't figure it out. The Keeper is not one to work with others."

"No," Sylvie agreed.

"I remember as a little girl," said Laurel, "we had a neighbor with a farm the next hill over from us. He hated everybody. I couldn't understand why. There's probably a little of him in the Keeper of the Cave."

"What was he like?"

"We didn't have much to do with him, except my father had him build us a few things—a ladder, I think, and a stile. He was very good with his hands."

Sylvie thought. "The Keeper has been building something too. Cages, I assume. There were all these wood chips on the ground."

Their talk was interrupted by the squawk of an orange bird in a persimmon tree. Then a grumpy frog croaked loudly, "Booook oooopen!" and the sky lifted away. All of a sudden a boy was looking down into the story. He couldn't have been more than fifteen years old.

Where'd he *come from?* thought Sylvie as she ran to get to her place in Chapter One. She arrived at the first scene just as the boy began reading. Finding her mark, she spoke out boldly to the king: "Father," she declared as always, "I cannot marry Prince Riggeloff."

King Walther was about to reply when a girl's voice called out: "Matty! How do you like my book?"

"I'm just starting it," said the boy. His voice was changing and sounded a bit wobbly. "Give me a chance."

A pretty girl of maybe eleven appeared overhead. She looked like Kara's kid sister, if Kara had one. Her short-ish hair was held to the side with a blue barrette. "Oh, yeah," she said, looking over his shoulder. "Just wait till you meet Riggeloff."

"Where are you off to?" he said.

"Making lunch for Winky Dink. You know how kids are when they're hungry."

"I know how *he* is."

"I figure we should keep the little monster happy."

"Just keep him away from sharp objects."

"Oh, let me see your arm. Is it better?"

"You can hardly tell. Kind of amazing how fast cuts heal these days."

"I'd like to box Wink's ears."

"Don't," said the boy. "He'll just go after *you*."

She sighed. "A shame we had to shut down the Performance and Affect Monitor. He seemed to be getting better."

"I wanted to keep PAM going, but we have to conserve electricity."

"Uh-huh," said the girl, heading off to the galley.

The boy frowned into the book and started reading again. Princess Sylvie and the other characters tried not to look up, but how could they help it? It *couldn't* be the astronaut Matt, but clearly it was—drastically younger than he'd been the last time they saw him. And what had happened to Kara? The twenty-nine-year-old exobiologist was now in early adolescence. What would *Wink* look like?

Sylvie and the others stumbled through their lines as best they could until Kara's high voice called out that lunch was ready. Matt left the book floating over his workstation.

King Walther gave his daughter a grim nod. "We need to have a meeting," he said.

Minutes later Sylvie led Norbert Fangl, Laurel, and Rose down the torchlit corridor.

"Where are you going?" A sharp female voice cut through the dimness.

"Mother!" Sylvie cried. "Um, we're just going to see Father."

"And what, may I ask," she said, fixing Rosetta with her most queenly look, "are you staring at, Miss Stein?"

"Oh, um, I was just admiring . . ." She seemed not to

know what to call the thing the queen had on her head.

"My new crown?"

"Yes! Lovely!"

"The royal physician designed it." She turned her head to the side to give Sylvie's friends a better look. Instead of her regal upward-pointing crown, she wore a strange, wide-brimmed affair, a sort of gem-encrusted farm hat.

"The *doctor* designed this?" said Sylvie.

"Remarkable, isn't it?" The queen smiled thinly. "It's to reduce my perfidious vision."

"Perhaps you mean your *peripheral* vision, Your Majesty?" Fangl suggested gently.

"Something of that sort. It's done wonders for me."

"It's certainly, as you say, remarkable," said Sylvie. "We must run, though. Father calls. Good to see you up and around."

The queen inclined her head slightly to give Sylvie and the others leave to leave.

"What do you make of it?" Sylvie murmured to Rosetta as they hurried on.

"The hat? I mean crown?"

"I'd guess," said Fangl, "it's to keep her from seeing too much. Especially to keep her from looking up."

By the time they entered the council room, King Walther and several senior advisers were already seated, including the rotund Chief Councillor and the aged Warburton. The king thumped his scepter and got to the point. "You all saw what just happened in the spaceship," he said. "Does anyone understand it? Warburton?"

Warburton, whose prominent forehead cast the lower part of his face in shadow, had little to suggest. "Clearly a spell," he said at last, stroking his chin. "Perhaps this unseen passenger, the one they call Pam, is a sorceress."

The king had begun nibbling his mustache. "Very possible," he said. He nodded at Laurel. "Yes, my dear?"

"I think Mr. Fangl may have a thought," she said quietly.

"Fangl," said King Walther.

"Your Highness, I know that there are magical creatures in your kingdom. And we all know that the Keeper of the Cave is under a spell right up until the end of the story. But that sort of thing is much less common, I believe, in the space program."

"If you have a point," said the king, "I suggest you make it."

Fangl cleared his throat. "Well, Sire, I see two possible explanations, one of them better than the other. The first involves the theory of relativity, of which I'm sure you've heard."

The councillors looked at one another and then at the king, who nodded vaguely. "Go on."

"Well, one part of it is the idea that time and space are related, and the faster one moves, the slower time passes, until one reaches the speed of light . . ."

"The speed of what?" growled Warburton.

". . . beyond which time begins to move backward."

"What is he talking about?" muttered the Chief Councillor.

"The speed of night," said the king.

"On the other hand," Fangl went on, "it could be the air."

Now the councillors were thoroughly confused.

"But air," ventured the king, "is just . . . air."

"Air is many things, Sire. It contains many elements. The air they're breathing in the spaceship derives from ice taken from the moon we visited some time ago. We have no idea what contaminants may be in it."

The room grew silent. Finally Warburton thrust forward his chin and spoke. "No," he said. "It's the sorceress."

"Hear, hear," agreed another councillor, who began expounding on ways the malevolent creature named Pam might be dealt with.

Laurel touched Fangl's sleeve. "Sorry," she murmured. He smiled weakly.

After the meeting Fangl, Sylvie, and Laurel walked outside by the moat. Lilies blanketed much of the water's surface. "If it is the air," Fangl mused, shaking his head, "I don't know what we can do. They have to breathe."

"I don't understand," said Sylvie. "How could air make time go backward?"

"It doesn't. It has nothing to do with time. It has to do with patterns of cell generation."

"Patterns of . . . ?"

"Something is reversing the aging process. And it's doing it very quickly."

Laurel nodded. "No wonder they're bringing back so much of that water. It would cause a sensation on

Earth." She noticed Sylvie's puzzled look. "You probably can't understand that. You haven't aged since you were written, back in 1917."

"Princess," explained Fangl, "those who are not fortunate enough to live inside of a book are compelled to get older."

"I lived to be a very old woman on the outside," said Laurel, "before I came in here and became twelve again."

"I remember," said Sylvie. "That was a good day."

"The best," Laurel agreed, giving her favorite character a push.

Apparently, Matt liked *The Great Good Thing*. He read it several times before Kara demanded it back, claiming it was hers. For a week the book's characters were on call at all hours. Wink, who looked to be about seven years old, sometimes peeked at it, but he wasn't interested in that "dumb princess stuff."

Young attention spans have limits, however. Before long the astronauts got into a jag playing magnetic checkers, and Kara tossed the book in her cubby. She forgot about it for weeks, perhaps much longer. Sylvie didn't mind, because she had her hands full in the kingdom. There was the wedding to avoid, the animals to find, and Rose's suitors to control.

The recovery of the animals seemed a hopeless project. Godric and Thomas had agreed to confront the Keeper of the Cave; but in the end Thomas had to go alone, because Godric and the old Keeper could never appear

on the same page together. They were like strong mag-
nets sharing the same field. Turned one way, they
repelled each other. Turned the other way, they *became*
each other.

Thomas returned from his mission to Humped
Mountain with bruises but without information. He had
seen the wood shavings Sylvie had described but had no
luck getting the old man to say what he'd been building.

Godric placed a hand on Thomas's shoulder. "You
would think," he said, "that I'd know what was going
through his mind, but I don't."

"That's all right," said Thomas.

The rivals walked away together as Sylvie and Laurel
watched. Norbert Fangl was just coming up, rubbing an
apple he'd bought from the peddler. "They're getting
along better," he said.

"So it seems," said Sylvie.

He leaned over the edge of the drawbridge and took a
bite. "I think if it weren't for this rivalry over Miss Stein,
they could be great friends."

All at once the castle rocked slightly and the water
sloshed about in the moat. A frog started to croak,
"Boook . . ." but got swamped by a wave. The sky
opened partway, then flopped back down again, as if a
clumsy person was trying to open the book. The sky lifted
again, and this time it stayed off. Somewhere a baby was
fretting.

"Here's that book," came the voice of a young boy.
"Maybe it'll help."

"What? Oh!" A little girl, maybe four years old,

peeped over the edge of the page. She picked up the book, and as she did Sylvie got a better look at her. The girl was wearing one of Kara's T-shirts, only it went all the way to the floor, like a nightgown.

"Can you read it to him," said the boy, "while I go pick some wheatgrass in the lab?"

Sylvie, astonished, watched the girl's mouth curl down and her eyes lower.

"What?" the boy said impatiently.

The girl blinked away a tear. "I . . ."

"Come on, Kara. What is it?"

"I don't think I can anymore."

"Can't what?" said the boy. "Read? Sure you can." His eyes narrowed as he looked at the girl more closely. "You've been getting younger again, haven't you?"

"So've you."

"I can still read."

The girl's face crumpled into tears. "So *what*? So what, you big doody!"

"Hey, hey," he said quietly. "I didn't mean anything . . ."

"I can't *read* anymore, Matty!" she wailed. "What's happening to me?"

"It's the air. Remember, Kara? You remember what happened to the lab mice."

She nodded. "They got teeny and died." Sylvie could see the top of the girl's head thump against Matt's shoulder. Her sobs seemed to affect the baby, because soon a loud wail filled the cabin.

"Come on," said Matt, who was not that far from tears himself, "Wink needs us."

The girl rubbed her hands over her face and took a ragged breath. "'Kay."

"Don't worry," he said. "We'll figure this stuff out."

She disappeared, then came back holding a red-faced infant.

"Careful he doesn't bite you," Matt cautioned.

"He doesn't have teeth anymore."

"That's one good thing. Here, I'll read a little. You have a good hold on him?"

She looked at him and did her best to smile. "I can still hold a baby, Matt."

"Good girl."

"You silly-head."

The children strapped themselves in and got comfortable as Matt started to read *The Great Good Thing*. He was no longer as good at reading as he used to be and stumbled over the hard words, but he kept at it. Soon the baby's crying tapered off.

"It's working, Matty," the girl whispered.

He forged on, his voice growing confident. By the time he reached the part where Riggeloff's thieves cast the Shawls of Slumber over the guards, Kara and little Wink were fast asleep. The boy laid the book down and just looked at them. He had the delicate face of a six-year-old but the sad eyes of a middle-aged man. It about broke Sylvie's heart to watch. She was sure he understood what was happening to them. No doubt he knew that the time was coming when he would no longer understand, no longer be able to take care of the younger ones, or himself.

Laurel whispered, "They're like a little family, aren't they?"

Sylvie nodded. "Even Wink looks peaceful."

"He'll be the first to die."

Sylvie gave Laurel a horrified look. "I thought people got *old* and died."

"That's the usual way," Laurel agreed. "But things are a little backward here."

"What will happen?"

"Do you want to know?"

"I want to help."

"But you can't."

Sylvie gave her a straight look. "Just tell me what will happen, please."

Laurel nodded. "Well, if he gets much younger, his lungs won't be fully developed. He'll have trouble taking in air. That will be painful." She paused. "It may also be terrifying."

"Poor baby," moaned Sylvie.

"His other organs will be less developed too. His heart, kidneys . . ."

Sylvie was staring at the sleeping infant. Two of his little fingers were in his mouth.

"I'm afraid he will suffer," Laurel concluded.

Sylvie walked off by herself a little way, staring at the lilies below the drawbridge. Then she came back. "How long," she said, looking at Laurel and Fangl, "before it starts?"

"Soon, I would think."

"I want to go in," said Sylvie.

Laurel looked alarmed. "What do you mean?"

"Go in. Take it on. Take it over from him so he doesn't have to do it."

"How would you do that?"

"Enter his dreams. I've done it with other people."

"Not with infants. What if he doesn't have dreams? Sylvie, don't try this."

"It's the way I was written. You of all people should know that."

"I know," she cried, "but I didn't mean . . . this!"

"I know you made me who I am. But what I do is up to me. You've said so yourself."

"I take it back!"

"Look at him," she said, nodding toward Wink. "Do you want him to suffer? Do you want him to be terrified?"

"Sylvie, you've never died before. You might not come back."

Sylvie looked at her Author. How she loved this strange girl with the dark blue eyes. "I'm not asking for your permission," she said. "I'm asking for your help."

"Help you how? I don't know of any way for you to enter his mind."

"Are you sure? Look over there to the east. What do you see?"

"See? Where?"

"At the end of the kingdom."

"I don't see anything."

"Tell the truth. An Author has to be honest with her characters."

"It may not be anything."

"It's a forest, Laurel. A forest like our forest, but different."

"Maybe."

"Little Kara is having a dream about our story."

"What if she is? It's not her mind you want to enter."

"No, but right now she's feeling very protective of Wink. The border between her mind and his is very thin."

Laurel's eyes rounded with alarm.

"It should be possible to cross from her to him," said Sylvie.

"I forbid you."

"You can't. You gave me free will."

"You would *disobey* me?"

Sylvie's heart was beating fast. She had seldom argued with Laurel and had never defied her. In over a hundred years the question of power had never come up. She took a step back from the brink. "Come on," she said gently. "Let's go over and just take a look. Maybe it's not even possible."

Laurel paused. "I suppose we can do that," she said. "Coming, Mr. Fangl?"

The geometer had been looking back and forth from creator to character. He nodded.

The three of them took the cobbled street that led out of town. None of them spoke while they crossed the sheep pasture and entered the forest, following a well-worn footpath. They were still some distance from the eastern boundary when a servant on horseback caught up with them. He was a heavyset young fellow and nearly fell off when he attempted to swing down from the saddle. He bowed awkwardly. "Your Highness!"

Sylvie gave him no more than a glance. "What is it?"

"His Highness would like Your Highness to return at once to the castle."

"My father wants me back at the castle?"

The servant stammered. "Not that Highness, Your Highness. Prince Pingree."

"You're joking, yes?"

The poor fellow bowed even lower. "Never, Your Highness."

Sylvie looked at him and nodded. "I believe you."

Fangl scratched the back of his neck and smiled. "It would seem, Princess, that your fiancé doesn't entirely trust you."

"What does he think I'm going to do? Leave the kingdom?" She stopped herself. That was exactly what she was planning to do.

"I saw him on the parapet before," Fangl murmured in her ear. "Perhaps he, too, has noticed the new forest to the east."

Sylvie turned to the messenger. "You may tell the prince that I will come home when it suits me."

The poor fellow bowed even lower, till his forehead brushed the path. "His Highness expected you might say that. And he instructed me to say, in that case, that he is not requesting that you return. He is *ordering* you to return."

"I see." Sylvie turned to her friends. "Well, shall we continue?" She strode on down the path, leaving the confused messenger by himself.

"What a lovely husband Mr. Pingree will make," said Laurel with a smile.

"You created him," said Sylvie. "You have only yourself to blame."

"Wait!" The servant ran after them. "You have to come back with me!"

"Actually," said Princess Sylvie, "I don't." She turned and continued on.

"But I'll be flogged!"

Sylvie turned briefly and called to him. "Then I suggest you get a better master."

Gradually, the path ahead grew less well defined, the brambles thicker. Few people came this close to the border. The friends pressed on and emerged from a tangle of bushes to find a bare white strip running from south to north.

"Here we are," said Fangl. "The margin."

They peered across, trying to get a sense of the dream on the other side. It was a mirror image of the forest they'd come from. Kara was certainly an accurate dreamer. Even without knowing more about her, you could predict she'd grow up to be a scientist. The only thing she'd left out was the sound of crickets. Apparently, Kara hadn't noticed the crickets in *The Great Good Thing* and so hadn't dreamed about them. Her dream forest was silent.

"It looks easy enough," Sylvie said. "I'll just cross her mind and see if there's a border with the baby on the other side. If there isn't, I'll come right back."

Fangl looked at her gravely. "Don't dally, Princess. Kara's dream is your bridge back home. If she wakes up while you're in her mind . . ."

A trumpet note reached them from somewhere back in the kingdom. It was soon followed by a commotion of horses plunging through the underbrush.

Fangl compressed his lips. "I think Prince Pingree didn't care for the answer you gave his messenger."

"Too bad," Sylvie said with a short laugh. "What is he going to do? Arrest me?"

"A foolish idea, Princess, but it wouldn't be his first."

"You're right. I'd better go."

"I don't like this," said Laurel. "No one has ever attempted a double crossing before. Crossing any mind-field can be treacherous. Crossing *two* of them . . ."

"I'll be careful."

The crashing of branches grew louder, accompanied by shouts.

"Princess Sylvie!" rang out a voice like a splinter. It was Pingree himself, not taking any chances with messengers.

"That's my cue," Sylvie said.

Laurel gave her a stricken look. "What if I don't see you again?"

"If that happens," said Sylvie, "I will be unhappy forever."

"Go!" said Fangl as the first of the horsemen broke through into the open.

"There she is!" cried Pingree, on the second horse.

In the flick of a moment Sylvie hopped across the margin and disappeared into Kara's dream.

chapter twelve

The shouts and hoofbeats faded as Sylvie ran on through the woods. Finally, sure she was not followed, she slowed to a walk, taking in a landscape much like the one she'd left, yet different, as a copy is different from the original.

The path took a turn, and Sylvie was stunned to find her way blocked by an enormous tortoise, its head swiveling slowly to face her. *Her* tortoise! "So *there* you are!" She ran up to the creature only to find that she passed right through him. It was Kara's dream of Kara's faltering memory of the tortoise, not the tortoise itself.

"Oh!" Sylvie moaned, hugging herself sadly.

She continued. The image of a blind owl flew high over the image of the forest, and Sylvie's sadness deepened. Would she never see her creatures again?

Never mind, she thought. *Keep going. Get to the other side. How wide is this dream, anyway?*

She emerged from the woods to find herself at the edge of a playing field. There were no such places in her book, and she'd never heard of a game like this.

Two teams of ten each faced each other. Prince Riggeloff led one team, which was dressed in black uniforms. Kara—a grown-up Kara, her hair flying—captained the other. She was running down the field with her teammates, all kicking a leather-covered ball, passing it with their feet from one to another. The opposing team, meanwhile, tried to kick the ball away.

"Watch out!" Sylvie cried, noticing that several of Riggeloff's men were carrying nets. As they ran they slung the nets over first one, then another of Kara's teammates, sending them instantly to sleep. Soon there was only Kara herself, weaving in and out of the opposing team, trying to keep control of the ball as she ran.

Sylvie's instinct was to run out there and help. But she remembered this was Kara's dream, not hers. Sylvie's mission lay in what remained of Wink's mind, somewhere to the east.

She hurried on, looking back as she went. Kara was struggling valiantly, but—was it possible?—she seemed to be getting shorter. Soon the girl was only three times the size of the ball, then twice the size. She was too small to kick it and had begun pushing it with two hands down the field. Riggeloff's men circled her, laughing.

Don't help her! Sylvie told herself sternly. *It's a nightmare. She'll wake up soon enough.*

Sylvie fell into a loping run as the field gave way to low, shrub-covered hills and then more woods. Here, on the far side of Kara's dream, not all details were filled in. Trees were implied, leaves lost in an upward vagueness, the path no more than a sketch. The border couldn't be far.

When she got there, she almost didn't recognize it. There was only a bulging mist ahead of her, white as cream. She stopped and listened. Out of the fog came the strangled cry of an infant. Sylvie took a breath to calm herself.

Laurel warned me not to do this. What if . . . The cry grew abruptly louder, and Sylvie didn't think anymore, but stepped straight into the whiteness.

It didn't have the feel of a dream. She was in a *mind*— a mind nude of ideas, memories, hopes, and thoughts. She shuddered. This wasn't a clean, well-lighted place, but cramped, dim, and . . . sticky.

Does anyone live here?

Then she thought: *I do. I have to.*

I am Wink.

And with that, she took possession of the emptied mind of the child. The effect was immediate. Pain gripped her throat, her head, the nerves of her body. She sank to her knees, barely noticing the rubbery floor beneath her. The fog surrounding her was a sort of electrical cloud. Brief flashes—nerve signals, pain signals— illuminated the slippery walls, and each flash sent a new shock through her body.

I do this for you, little one. Go quickly now!

Wink cried out again, but the voice was no longer his, it was Sylvie's, as a new and excruciating pain gripped her intestines. All her systems were failing at once, her heart flittering in her chest like a frightened bird. She rolled about in the slimy dimness.

"Wink! Wink!"

A child's voice was calling.

"It's all right, Wink. Here, let me hold you."

The spongy cave suddenly lit up as two windowlike openings let in painful shafts of light.

"He's awake, Matt! Hello, Winky. We love you."

Flinching, Sylvie forced herself to look out. There was little four-year-old Kara making cooing sounds.

Sylvie had a terrible realization: Kara was out there! She had woken from her dream! The bridge back to the book was broken. Sylvie was Wink now, and as Wink, she would die.

So this is what it's like to be one of them, she thought. *To be human.*

"Here's the book, Matty. Go ahead."

"Okay," said the voice of a young boy. "Where should I start?"

"Anywhere!"

"Okay, here goes. 'It was a cloudless dawn, and the Mere was calm. Reflected in its surface, the blind owl circled overhead, with a white mouse dangling from its yellow beak.'"

"I think he's listening, Matty. Keep going."

The light began to dim as the baby's eyesight failed. The children were visible now through a vague film. Sylvie began hallucinating. She imagined she saw the astronaut named Wink as a young man standing before her. He looked at her with calm eyes. It was a wonderful look, quietly grateful. He nodded to her briefly and faded into the fog.

"'The great bird flew west over the mountain, passing the shepherds' huts in the high fields, and arrived at last at the castle. Circling the turret, it swooped down to the balcony outside the princess's chamber. It cocked its head questioningly. Princess Sylvie always opened the window at first light to offer it food and murmur secrets that it didn't understand; but there was no sign of her today, and the window was locked tight.'"

Sylvie listened as if her life depended on it. She recognized the words, of course. They were her own story, being read to her now by a child. Her mind grew confused, and she felt herself losing her hold on consciousness. She fought against it. *Keep reading,* she thought. *Keep me alive.*

But how could she stay alive? She who was supposed to live forever was dying at the moment of birth.

Help! Sylvie cried from the flickering depths. She struggled to take in air, but her lungs were not developed enough. She was starting to suffocate!

And then, another hallucination. She sensed a presence beside her and made out the outline of a person holding out a hand. A great calmness filled the chamber.

From the slime of the floor, Sylvie groaned. Her heart beat feebly. She wanted desperately to reach out her hand, but she had no strength.

The being moved closer. That was when Sylvie recognized her. It was her friend, the girl with the dark blue eyes. She was beckoning.

No, it was too hard. Sylvie felt a great dizziness sweeping her away. She couldn't fight so strong a pull.

The girl smiled, her arm outstretched.

This time Sylvie forced herself to lift her hand.

Their fingers touched.

chapter thirteen

Sylvie frowned. Her body felt clammy. Slowly, she opened her eyes to find herself in her canopied bed in the castle, the sheets soaked with sweat.

"She's waking up!" cried Mary, the queen's round-faced attendant.

Faces crowded around, even the castle's resident priest, who'd been summoned in case things went badly.

"Dear child!" cried the queen, bending over the bed to embrace her. Her new wide-brimmed crown poked Sylvie in the cheek.

The royal physician began shooing people out. "Come, come, everybody," he said. "We must let her rest."

Sylvie nodded gratefully. Her eyelids closed. Time passed dreamlessly. She had no idea how long she slept, but after a while she began to feel a presence in the room and opened her eyes.

"Hi," said the girl with the dark blue eyes.

"Laurel," Sylvie whispered. She remembered where she had seen her last. "How did you . . . ?"

"How did I reach you? Not hard. Once the boy began reading our story and you began listening to it, I was able to cross from the book into your mind—well, into that poor baby's mind."

"By then he was gone," said Sylvie. "It was only me."

"It looks like I got there just in time."

The two friends gave each other a long look.

"I almost lost you," Laurel said.

Sylvie nodded. "You did lose me. You pulled me back from the dead."

Laurel closed her eyes briefly. "Well," she said, giving her head a shake, "are you feeling well enough to hear the news around here?"

"All right."

"Which do you want to hear about, the wedding or the funeral?"

"If the wedding is mine, I'll take the funeral."

"The wedding *is* yours. The funeral's Wink's. The children have decided to release him into the universe. They're working out some kind of service now. I think they want to read from our book."

"That's very sweet."

"It is. But your Mr. Fangl is planning to disrupt it."

"That doesn't sound like him."

"Not ordinarily, but there's a message he feels he has to get to them."

"What could be that important?"

Laurel went to the door. "Let him tell you. He's been wanting to talk to you since you got home."

Norbert Fangl peeped around the door. "May I come in?"

"Please," said Sylvie.

He stepped in. "It's good to see you so much better."

"Thank you, Fangl. I understand you have news for me."

The geometer examined his shoes. "Well, Your Highness," he said, "put in its simplest terms, the children are juvenescing too quickly."

"They're *what*?"

"Losing age. Are you sure you're well enough to talk about this?"

"Yes, yes, go on."

"Well, if we take the four-year figure for their loop around Jupiter, our young astronauts will have regressed to Mr. Winkermann's unfortunate condition seven months before arriving at Earth."

"Oh no!"

"Quite. What I would suggest to them is that they do a little less breathing. Well, a lot less breathing."

"It sounds impossible."

"Yes, but mountain climbers manage to breathe very thin air. I would like our friends to think of themselves as mountain climbers."

"How are you going to tell them this?"

"I've already made changes in the text they are planning to read at Mr. Winkermann's funeral. I would have waited to consult with you, but you were . . ."

"Dead."

"Well, dead tired."

Princess Sylvie nodded. "Let's hope it works."

She would have liked to talk more—the plan was intriguing—but her eyes kept closing. She hadn't realized how much sleep it takes to waken the dead.

The children had done what they could. They'd wrapped the baby's body in a white T-shirt like a shroud, with only Wink's head poking out, and had laid him inside an escape hatch. Little Kara, not having flowers, had tucked some fresh wheatgrass in a fold of the shirt and combed the baby's hair.

As Princess Sylvie and other characters watched from the open page, Kara switched on a cassette player. The sound of a Bach cello suite filled the cabin.

Matt, holding *The Great Good Thing*, looked at Kara and cleared his throat. "We're here," he began quietly, "to say good-bye to a man . . . I mean kid. Person."

He frowned, determined not to lose his thought. "Wink had some big problems, but he couldn't help it. For a while it looked like he was getting better, but then he stopped taking the medicine. Not even the Performance and Affect Monitor can help you if you don't take your medicine."

He paused. For a small boy, he had already made a big speech.

"There's a part of this book that made Kara and me think about how it might be for him getting close to heaven and seeing heaven coming to meet him." His voice faltered, and he had to wait several seconds before going on.

"Anyway, here it is." He cleared his throat. "'A distant sound reached her, and she strained to hear. Drums, and yes, the tinny bleat of far-off trumpets. She climbed out the window onto the stone balcony, but **breathe less coud s noting umls and muicin.**'"

Matt stared at the page before him, then shook his head and went on: "'Then she thought she detected a faint glimmer in the morning light. Gradually, it grew, and she made out little banners and horses, and in the front of them jugglers and **shut down machine by two thirds e se c see em lealy, ulttud, much cloer o shuig an alkng hile ugles.**'"

Matt stammered and stopped. "What the heck?" He looked at Kara accusingly. "Have you been messing around with the book?"

"I haven't touched it, Matty, I swear!"

"But . . ." He looked at the strange words. "It says . . . Gosh, Kara, the book is telling us to turn down the evaporation machine!"

"But it couldn't say that!"

"I know!"

She looked at him with rounding eyes. "It's God," she whispered. "It's a message from God."

"Whatever it is, we better do it."

"Yes, yes! Quick!"

Matt stopped himself from rushing off. He looked at the infant in the escape hatch. "Let's finish."

Kara put her hand over her mouth.

"So," said Matt, "have a great trip, Wink."

"We love you, Winky." Kara gave the baby a kiss on the forehead. Then she stepped back, and Matt closed the air lock.

"Good-bye," he whispered. He paused a long moment, then pushed the button that shot the tiny shrouded figure into space.

They watched through the window until Wink dwindled to a white dot and disappeared among the billions of dots in the Milky Way.

Then the children ran to adjust the air machine.

Sylvie had put off this day as long as possible, but the time had come for her to keep her promise and marry the despicable Pingree. Everyone was in their brightest array and their darkest mood—except, of course, the triumphant jester, who bounced around the great hall checking on flower arrangements and sampling pastries and mulled wine. The ceremony was still hours away, but he was out of control with self-satisfied delight.

Sylvie kept to her chamber with Rosetta and several servants, making adjustments to the wedding gown. She had chosen, finally, a simple dress of ivory satin on which she'd had embroidered—white on white—representations of her three magic animals. The only touch of color was the circlet of violets she wore as a crown.

"You can still escape," murmured Rosetta as she worked on the puff of Sylvie's sleeve.

"I'd love to, but only with the owl flying overhead, and the tortoise crawling through the forest, and the fish back in the Mere. It doesn't look as though those things are going to happen."

"Thomas and Godric are out there looking."

Sylvie sighed. "That's the one good thing to come out of this."

"They aren't enemies anymore," said Rosetta, nodding.

"Let's hope they remember that when it comes time for you to choose between them."

"Do I need to?"

Sylvie looked at the tall shepherdess with the remarkable hair. "I don't know. What do you think?"

Rosetta looked down, smiling slightly. "I think," she said, "we should deal with your situation first."

"We are. We're admitting defeat."

A soft knock on the door made them look up. A moment later Laurel glided in. "How's it coming?"

"Terrible," said Sylvie. "I'm getting married." She nodded at the two young maidservants working on the train. "Thank you both," she said. "I won't be needing you for a while."

They gave her a pitying smile. As they left, Prince Godric poked his head in.

"Come in," said Sylvie. "Maybe you can cheer us up."

"Any news?" said Rosetta.

Godric bowed to Sylvie and blushed at Rose. "I'm afraid not," he said. "Thomas and I have been combing the kingdom."

The girl with the dark blue eyes went to the window and looked out over the valley to the mountain. "I keep thinking," she said to herself, "the key to this must lie with the Keeper of the Cave."

"He was no help at all," said Godric. "He even attacked Thomas."

"A shame," said Laurel, "that you can't read his mind. You'd think you could. After all, at the end of the story he turns *into* you."

"I know, but I can't stand him. I don't *want* to know what he's thinking."

"Not even to save Princess Sylvie?" said Rosetta, stepping forward. She smiled. "Not even for me?"

Godric swallowed hard.

"You and the Keeper," said Laurel gently, "are two sides of the same mountain. Is there no way you can tell us what's on the other side?"

The prince groaned. "I don't want to."

"If you could only think about him differently," Laurel went on. "He does have some good qualities, you know."

"That horror?"

"You won't let yourself see them, but yes."

The prince looked at her uncertainly. "Are you taking his side?"

"Maybe we should stop thinking about sides. There's only one mountain, no matter how many sides it has."

"I'll stay on my own side, if you don't mind."

"But you can't," Laurel said. "You and he keep turning into each other. You need each other."

"I *need* him?"

Laurel seemed to be deciding how to put this. "He could certainly use some of your gentleness. You could use some of his power."

Godric looked hurt. "You're saying I'm weak?"

"Gentleness is not weakness," Sylvie broke in. "I'm sure she didn't mean that. But you can be a little . . . whiny sometimes."

His gaze fell. "Oh."

"See what I mean?" said Sylvie.

"I can't help it if my feelings get hurt."

"On the other hand," Laurel continued, "you have a capacity for love, and that's a great good thing."

"Yes, I have that," he said, glancing at Rosetta.

"He's good at making things, though. You've never made anything in your life."

"I have servants to make things."

"If you could build anything you wanted," Laurel went on, "make it with your own hands, what would it be?"

"I—I don't know." He turned away, holding his head in his hands. Suddenly a deep voice came out of him: "*He* can't make anything! That prancing puppy!"

Rosetta and Sylvie looked at each other.

"Which of you is speaking?" said Laurel quietly.

He turned around. It was Godric, his face flushed with fear. "I didn't say anything."

Rosetta raised a cautionary hand. "We should leave him alone."

"You were telling me what you would make," Laurel coaxed, ignoring Rosetta, "if, say, all you had was a sharp little hatchet."

"Nothing! Nothing!"

"Tell us."

"No, I . . . Something *useful*," he growled suddenly, his voice deeper, his forehead beginning to bulge. "Something a person could use!" He clutched his head. His shoulders were starting to bulk up. "But *he* wouldn't know about that." The voice was getting dangerously deep. His head turned away. "*He* wouldn't want to get his silk pants dirty making something like a stile or—" He whirled around to face the young women. His eyes were wild, and a wound glowed on his forehead. *"Why are you tormenting me?"*

"Sylvie! Quick!" cried Laurel.

Overcoming her revulsion, Princess Sylvie sprang forward, clasped the Keeper of the Cave by the shoulder, and planted a kiss on his wound.

The creature swayed, dizzy, as his distorted body began to straighten.

"Let him sit down!" said Rosetta sharply. "I think you're cruel to put him through this, Laurel."

But Laurel was not listening. "He said something about a stile."

"I don't know what that is," Sylvie said.

"Stile? A stile is a set of wooden steps that you set out by a fence, to help you climb over."

"Is there anything in the kingdom," said Sylvie slowly, "that you'd need help to climb over?"

Rosetta's eyes flashed. "I think you're both heartless!" She turned to Godric, who was slumped in a plum-colored chair looking dazed. "You don't have to answer any more questions," she said, holding his chin and looking in his eyes.

"We know you don't need a stile to get over the margin," Laurel said.

"No, I've crossed it lots of times," Sylvie agreed.

"But you might need one to get to the extreme front of the book, or the back, if there were an index, which there isn't."

"But we've been to the front before," Sylvie countered. "Remember when we had to borrow some *d*s from the acknowledgments page?"

"Yes, but did you get any farther?"

"Isn't that the front of the book?"

"Not quite. You're forgetting the copyright page."

"The what?"

"Not to mention the title page. These are pages where the characters never go."

The girls shared a clear look.

"Are you coming, Rosetta?" cried Sylvie, starting for the door.

The shepherdess looked up. "I don't know," she said, tempted in spite of herself.

Laurel threw on her blue cloak.

"I'd better stay with the prince," Rosetta said. "He's still a little weak."

"Yes, fine," said Sylvie, lifting the hem of her dress and swooshing through the door. Her voice reached Rosetta from down the hall: "Don't let them start the wedding without us!"

Being weightless helped the girls move quickly, sailing over thickets of exposition rather than picking their way along, adverb by adjective. That was fortunate, since Sylvie's wedding dress tended to poof out in low gravity. It got snagged often enough as it was. The trickiest parts were the places where the jester had scribbled between the lines of the story. That didn't leave a lot of room.

"I knew he was keeping a journal," Laurel mused, glancing about, "but I didn't know he'd written so much. Do you see what he says here?" She nodded at Pingree's notes about the tax department. "He wants to build up the Treasury."

"What in the world for?" said Sylvie.

"Seems he wants to create an empire."

"Isn't it enough to have a kingdom?"

She took Sylvie's hand as they pushed off again. "Some people never have enough."

They paused to catch their breath beside the oversized *O* that starts Chapter Two. "I thought I'd give him just a touch of greed, to make him interesting," Laurel continued. "I didn't realize a little goes a long way."

"It does, doesn't it?"

The princess pushed off again with Laurel close

behind her. They floated back through Chapter One, eventually coming to rest amid the table of contents. There was nothing here that looked like a stile or a ladder, so they continued on to the dedication page. That was mostly white space.

"I don't know," said Sylvie.

"Don't give up. We've got a couple more pages to go," Laurel replied, heading to the left-hand margin.

They clambered over onto a page filled with thank-yous. At first they saw nothing. But then, tucked behind the boldface print of the word *Acknowledgments*, they found what they were looking for: a cunningly fashioned wooden stile lying on its side, half hidden by the curve of the *g*.

The excitement in Sylvie's eyes dimmed, and she grew thoughtful. "We haven't needed a stile so far," she said. "Without gravity, we can just float from section to section."

"There must be some use for it," said Laurel. "Maybe on the next page."

The friends glided over the left-hand margin onto a page filled with tiny print. Sylvie and Laurel had to get down on their hands and knees to fit between the lines. The words were mysterious. "What does this mean?" said Sylvie. "'. . . any resemblance to actual events . . .'"

"Don't worry about it. Keep looking."

"We have *lots* of actual events in our story."

"Ouch!" said Laurel, bumping her head on *coincidental.*

"My animals can't fit in here. I can hardly fit myself! Do you remember how *big* they are?"

"They're big in the imagination," Laurel replied. "But remember, *owl* is just a three-letter word."

They continued on, eventually crawling from the top of the page to the bottom and back up again. Sylvie's wedding dress was not meant for this and was constantly getting caught. An ISBN number tore the satin train.

"Oh, dear!"

"It's all right," said Laurel. "If we find what we're looking for, you won't be needing the dress."

"But they're not here!"

"They've got to be," said Laurel. "There's only the title page left."

"Could we have missed them somehow?"

Laurel paused to think. "Is there anything we can't see into?"

"There's that little circle."

"That's the copyright symbol. There's only a tiny *c* in there."

"Then there are those straight fence posts. I can't see past them."

"Fence posts? Oh, you mean *brackets*. That's true. I can't either, now that I'm a character. Characters aren't supposed to see through brackets. They're just for Readers."

Laurel suddenly realized what she'd said. Without a word, the girls approached the first bracket. It gleamed like steel, so different from the soft semicircle of a parenthesis. They tried floating over it but found they couldn't.

"Why can't we get *over* this?" cried Sylvie.

"It's almost like it's a different energy field," Laurel said. From the other side came a muffled beating sound. "I think I hear your owl!"

"You're right! Oh!" Sylvie tried vainly to bend the bracket. "We've got to get in!"

"Get the stile!"

They hurried to the margin and dragged the stile to the bracket. Sylvie was up it in a moment and was relieved to find she could see over the top. There they were, her wonderful animals, each wedged in a set of parentheses and caged by the outside brackets.

"They have no room!"

At the sound of her voice, the owl's wings beat fiercely. The tortoise extended its head partway from its shell. Only the fish remained motionless. It was dried out, rolled up like a proclamation and secured with a velvet ribbon. That was all right, Sylvie realized. It always went into hibernation when it was out of the water.

"We'll get you out, dear ones!"

Laurel was beside her at the top of the stile. "They're in there pretty tight," she mused. "But at least they're weightless."

"Do you think we could just lift them out?" said Sylvie.

The brackets remained unyielding, but the girls were able to reach down and pull up one set of parentheses, like tongs, lowering them onto an empty space on the page. The parentheses quickly fell away, revealing a very confused tortoise.

The girls pulled out the second set, then the third. The owl was a little frantic at first but calmed down under Sylvie's stroking and soft words. "Hush, little one. It's all right."

Had gravity prevailed, they might never have gotten the tortoise home. As it was, it wasn't difficult to guide the creature over the margin to the main part of the book. Sylvie then jumped onto his back, her tattered dress flowing out in all directions. Laurel glided alongside, carrying the rolled-up fish under her arm, while the owl circled overhead, crying, *"Screeck! Screeck!"*

Before long their odd parade was approaching the castle. Ahead, a solitary figure swayed toward them on a donkey.

"It's Mr. Fangl!" cried Laurel.

"Look what we found, Fangl!" Sylvie called out.

"Yes, yes, very good," said the geometer, trying to dismount without floating away. "But did you see just now when the book opened?"

"The book opened?" said Sylvie.

"Didn't you notice?"

"Actually, we've been outside the story. Saving our *animals.*" Sylvie felt a little annoyed that Fangl wasn't excited about this.

"Very nice, yes. But then you didn't notice the boy Matt."

"What about him?"

"His voice cracked."

Sylvie looked at Laurel in bewilderment. "Fangl, what *are* you talking about?"

"His voice cracked! Don't you see? He's senescing!"

"He's what?"

"Isn't it wonderful? He's getting *older*!"

PART FOUR

peanut butter and jelly

chapter fourteen

Prince Pingree called for another stoup of mulled wine to wash down his plate of dainties. He'd been sampling the slivered calves' brains, and they'd gone straight to his head.

The former jester looked like a Christmas ornament in his blue silk doublet and gold braid as he staggered through the grand hall bowing to confused footmen and offering toasts to the serving wenches. Princes don't bow to footmen, even princes who not long ago were commoners.

"Have you seen my bride?" he asked an alarmed-looking page.

"No, Sire," the lad answered, matching Pingree bow for bow.

"There, there, fear not, my boy. Prince Pingree will not harm thee."

"No, Sire."

"The prince looks kindly on all."

"Yes, Sire. Thank you, Sire."

Pingree turned to the queen, who had just entered with several ladies-in-waiting, all overdressed for the impending wedding. "Mother!" he declared in an unctuous voice, bowing yet again. "Have you seen my bride about?"

Queen Emmeline glared at him. "No, I haven't. And I would appreciate your *not* calling me by that name!"

"I quite agree," he said, swaying slightly and holding on to the guide ropes. "Much too formal. Shall I call you Mommy?"

"Oh!" The queen's eyes lifted to heaven.

"Mater? Dearest Mum?"

"'Your Highness' will do for now, until we can sort this out."

"Very good, Your Royal Motherness," he said, his words slurring. "But have you seen my intended?"

"What are you gabbling about?"

"The lovely Sylvie. My soon-to-be consort. My darling cherub." He paused to quaff his wine. "I need to work on these endearments."

"Anyone calling me?" rang out a gleeful voice.

Pingree swung around so suddenly, he swiveled right off his feet, landing on his skinny buttocks. "Where . . . ?" he said, dazed.

"Up here!"

Everyone stared as the princess floated through the window in the grip of the blind owl, her dress in torn streamers sailing out behind her.

Courtiers and servants alike burst into applause. Pingree looked aghast.

"My dearest Pingree!" cried Sylvie, as the owl released her and struggled into the air. "You're looking pale."

"Wh-Where," he stammered, "did you find him?"

"Same place as the others," came a different voice.

Pingree whirled around to see Laurel riding in atop the great tortoise. She held one end of a ribbon, at the other end of which, like a strange-looking balloon, floated the rolled-up fish.

"Wonderful!" cried Rosetta, her arm circled in Godric's.

For the first time in weeks Queen Emmeline smiled.

"Not fair!" cried Pingree, his mind still muddled with wine and calves' brains. "Not possible!"

"Don't fret, dearest," cooed Sylvie, floating over to him. "I know you don't love me or even like me. And I assure you my feelings for you are every bit as strong. But we mustn't think of ourselves. We'll have to forgo the misery of marriage and call the wedding off."

"No, no!"

"Yes, yes."

King Walther had come in toward the end of this exchange. He hurried to his daughter and folded her in his arms. "Thank heaven," he said simply.

"But, Father!" Pingree objected.

The king looked up. "What's that you said?"

"Well, aren't we father and son? Practically?" His eyes darted about. "Almost?"

"What we are," growled Walther, "are king and *insect*! Now get out of my sight before I have you stuffed in a catapult and flung in the moat!"

Pingree appealed to the stony-faced queen. "Mother," he said, "are you going to allow—"

She took a step toward him, and he took a step back.

Then two steps back. For a crazy moment it seemed they were doing a tango. Then he turned and fled the room.

A cheer went up.

"Don't you think, Father," said Sylvie brightly, "that it would be a shame to waste this wonderful food?"

"Quite right!" he said, catching her spirit. "I hereby declare the wedding canceled and the celebration begun!"

"Hear, hear!" cried the royal guards. In minutes the hall was loud with revelers. Additional wine casks were rolled in, followed by a great roasted boar garnished with eels' tongues, and the feasting began in earnest.

Sylvie was leading the tortoise outside when she ran into a serious-faced Norbert Fangl. "What is it?" she said, her smile fading.

"I can't help wishing, Your Highness," he said, "that our young astronaut friends could partake of this food."

"That's a wonderful thought, Fangl!"

"A shame they live in a different reality."

"How are they doing? Can you tell?"

"They're growing older, but they're growing thinner."

"Thinner?" She frowned. "How much thinner?"

Fangl glanced around at the feasting courtiers. "They're starving."

"But don't they have wheatgrass and Swiss chard and—?"

"They've got what they've got, but they're missing basic elements. Also, the continued weightlessness is hard on them. The calcium is leaching from their bones."

"Can they last until we reach Earth?"

"I don't have data on that."

Sylvie guided the great tortoise across the drawbridge while Fangl walked alongside. "You know," she said, "suddenly I don't feel hungry in the least."

"I'm sorry. I've spoiled your party."

She took his hand and kissed it. "No, dear Fangl. You just made me see that we're celebrating too soon. When our friends get back to Earth, we'll have a celebration that will shake the pages from the binding!"

"I'm sure we will, Your Highness. We *certainly* don't want any more funerals."

Kara's breath sounded wheezy and her movements were slow as she reached up, attempting to adjust the vents. She bit her underlip, determined not to make any more mistakes. Sylvie had seen her make several as the book floated unnoticed through the cabin.

"How's it going?" a male voice called out. A bearded young man came into view, panting audibly.

Sylvie noted with satisfaction that it was Matt, nineteen and all grown up. He looked kind of distinguished in a beard, she decided, although alarmingly thin.

"Not so good," said Kara. "Are you sure we can't get any more air in here?" She had the face of an underfed sixteen-year-old. Hunger had pared away the round cheeks she'd had when she was younger—a few weeks ago—leaving her gaunt. Her eyes, dark-rimmed, seemed too large for her face.

Matt touched her cheek. "We better not."

"I'm getting light-headed."

"That could be hunger."

"What a choice: starve or suffocate."

Matt watched her fumbling with the controls. "We only have two more weeks."

"Thirteen days, but who's counting?"

"Here, let me help you."

She sighed. "I don't know, Matt."

"What?"

"I can't breathe. I can't think. I don't know if I can do this."

"It'll be all right. They'll talk us down."

"If we last that long."

"We'll last."

"At least the fuel's holding out."

He nodded. "Using the moon water lightened the ship. Saved us a bunch of fuel."

"How much of that water is left?"

"The gauges say none."

She rubbed her forehead.

"Kara," he said soberly, "we've made it this far. We're not going to give up."

She leaned her head against his chest.

"And we're together," he murmured.

She nodded against him.

He gave a little laugh. "We even grew up together!"

"We did, didn't we? Boy, that was quick."

"It's like we're living cat years."

"You mean six or seven for every one year on Earth?"

"Now all we have to do," he said, his voice more serious, "is grow old together."

She lifted her head away and looked into his face. "Is that a proposal?"

He hesitated just a moment. "Kind of sounded like one, didn't it?"

"Get down on your knees and do it right."

"Can't. I'm weightless."

"All right, get *up* on your knees."

"What does that mean?"

"I have no idea. I told you I was fuzzy."

"You're beautiful."

"Oh, man," she said, laughing. "You're as fuzzy as I am."

He held her face between his hands. "So? Will you marry me?"

"Now, *that's* a proposal."

"It is. No mistaking it. What do you say?"

"I can't decide."

He bent forward and kissed her, gently and long.

"No fair," she said in a sort of whispered gasp.

"What isn't fair?"

"That it took you eight years to get around to it."

"Yeah," he whispered. "Think of all that time wasted."

"Let's not waste any more."

"Is that a yes?"

"Yes," she sighed, "it certainly yes is yes a yes."

"You *are* getting fuzzy."

"Yes."

"*Heartland*, this is Mission Control. Come in."

Silence.

"*Heartland*, do you read? This is Mission Control. Do you read? Come in, *Heartland*!"

Silence.

From their vantage point near the top of a half-open page, Sylvie and her friends looked around the cabin. No sign of life, except for blinking lights on the control panel, a regular beeping coming from somewhere, and ragged gasping sounds from the unconscious astronauts.

"They did all they could," said Fangl quietly.

Sylvie nodded. In the past two weeks she'd watched Kara and Matt struggle to stay alert. It was heart-wrenching to listen to their labored breathing as they followed instructions from Mission Control, making final adjustments to the ship's angle of approach to Earth's atmosphere.

Finally their own atmosphere began to dip below survivability level.

Matt used nearly the last of this strength to strap the already unconscious Kara into her seat. He managed to strap his own safety harness as well, then looked at her through dimming eyes. "Hang on, Kara," he whispered.

A terrible rasping sound came from her throat as her body fought to live.

"One more, Kara," he croaked. "One more breath. That's it."

He could do no more. His eyes closed. He did not see *The Great Good Thing* float down to the floor or a forgotten pair of pliers land on the workstation.

He lost consciousness before his weight regained the

gravity it had on Earth, and before it grew several times heavier than that, pressing his body into the seat. His heartbeats were slowing and becoming irregular. He never knew that the heat shield had begun shedding a plume of flame as the ship hurtled through the upper atmosphere like a fiery comet.

chapter fifteen

The characters in *The Great Good Thing* walked around in a daze. They felt as if their kingdom had suffered a national tragedy. Or maybe the opposite! It was terrible to be cut off from news of the outer world, just because the covers of the book were closed. Something great or else quite awful had happened, and they had no way of knowing which. All they knew for sure was that gravity was back. If you threw an apple in the air, it came down again.

Time went on, and the book remained closed. Fictional characters are like other people in that they can't stay indefinitely in a state of suspense. After a while they stopped thinking about the astronauts so much and went about their lives.

Pingree sneered down at them from his tower. He considered most of the characters subnormal for believing all this nonsense about stars. See where it had gotten Queen Emmeline, he thought. It drove her crazy. She'd recovered, finally, except for a distorted sense of fashion. Those hats!

Then there was this irritating business about marriage. Pingree had been so badly stung that he wanted to hear nothing more about the institution. And yet now, it seemed, Prince Godric and Rosetta Stein were planning a wedding! Pingree was the one who should be getting married, not those simpletons! He decided to keep to his room until it was over.

No one missed him. All were caught up in the excitement. Prince Riggeloff called off his pillaging, and the queen became almost gracious. At first people watched Thomas nervously, knowing that he, too, was in love with the tall shepherdess. It couldn't have been easy for him, but he had seen the way things were going between Rose and Godric and could hardly have been surprised.

And the prince was his friend. Godric had even asked Thomas to be his "best swain" in the wedding. Some courtiers objected, saying it wasn't right for an admitted thief to be given so prominent a role; but the prince prevailed.

He prevailed, but he didn't preside. In the days before the wedding some characters began whispering about Godric's frequent absences. He took long, solitary walks on woodland paths and along the slopes of Humped Mountain. The tailor found it hard to get him in for a fitting.

"Prewedding jitters, I guess," said Rosetta, when asked where Godric was keeping himself. Rosetta didn't have time for jitters. It was her idea, supported by Sylvie and Laurel, to hold the wedding outdoors by the Mere of Remind. Now that gravity had returned, the waterfall plunged down magnificently from the mountain, creating a crystalline explosion. There was no concern about bad weather, of course. Inside a book you always knew, on a given page, what the weather would be.

A week before the wedding Rosetta had quite a different ceremony to undergo—her investiture as a princess. A table covered with documents was brought down beside the Mere, and old Warburton began reading a proclamation while the parchment made soft crackling sounds in the breeze. The document was full of *wherefores* and *indissolubles* and dated *the fourth sundial of the nones of September, in the third indiction, in the 123rd year of the reign of King Walther.*

Then the priest, a wobbly fellow with a voice to match, began droning away in Latin. Then he said the same things in Lesser Old Middle High German, just to make sure, after which a small diamond-studded coronet was lowered onto Rosetta's head.

Trumpets rose gleaming in the sunlight and let forth a great flourish of congratulatory noise.

"Looks like your peasant days are over," murmured Sylvie, who stood beside her in a narrow-cut dress of ivory lace.

"A girl could get used to this!" whispered Rose. "Who'd think a simple girl from Croton Falls—"

"Rose," said Sylvie, "you've never been simple."

The exhilaration of now having *two* princesses was felt throughout the kingdom, and the feeling only increased as the wedding day approached.

The morning came, clear and cool. Rose and Sylvie were looking over the floral arrangements when

Laurel hurried to them. "The guests are starting to arrive. Time to get you into the tent." Rosetta and Sylvie, along with several handmaidens and flower girls, ducked into a blue silk tent at the rear of the crowd.

"But where . . . ?" Rosetta was looking through the tent flap at the crowd, which had begun taking their seats on velvet cushions set out on the grass.

"I'll go look for him," said Laurel, slipping away.

"Don't worry," said Sylvie, "he wants this wedding as much as you do."

"You're right. I won't think about it." But Rosetta kept peeking out the tent flap. "Where *is* that man?"

"Probably polishing his coronet," said Sylvie. "He'll be here. Breathe."

"You're right. Here I am a yoga teacher, holding my breath!" Rosetta closed her eyes, bending her head slightly and frowning in concentration. She began her deep breathing. "He better show up," she murmured between breaths.

"Shh. Keep breathing."

A few minutes later Laurel hurried in. "He's here!" Rosetta's eyes flew open. "Where?" She peered out.

"Up in front somewhere. When the music starts, you'll follow us down the aisle and meet him."

"Just like they do it back home," said Rosetta. "Except in my world my father would walk me down." A look of sadness flew across her face.

"May I act in his stead?" The flap lifted, and Norbert Fangl stood before them. He had obviously worked to improve his appearance. He even wore a soft hat of black velvet.

"I'd be honored," Rosetta said, slipping off her cape and giving her dress a discreet tug.

Just then a tapping of drums reached them and the sound of hautboys and mandolins playing a solemn air.

"That's us," said Sylvie. She lined up the candlelighter and ring bearer, then the three flower girls, giggly six-year-olds each carrying a basket of rose petals, and started them down the aisle.

"We're next," said Sylvie, nodding at Laurel. The two maidens of honor, bouquets in hand, ducked out from under the tent flap.

Behind them glided Rosetta, arm in arm with a benignly smiling Norbert Fangl. Rosetta's dress was spectacular, with swoops and swirls in various degrees of light blue. Aside from her tiara, she wasn't one for jewelry, but she made up for it in flowers. The crowd fell silent, except for an audible "Oooh!" from a lady-in-waiting.

Ahead, partly hidden from view, stood the priest and other officials. Prince Godric's glinting coronet was just visible.

"There he is!" Rosetta murmured under her breath.

Sylvie looked around at the excited faces of the courtiers and attendants. *This is the first wedding we've ever had in our book!* she realized. Then, as an afterthought: *Thank goodness it isn't mine.*

There was some kind of commotion up ahead. Sylvie saw one of the flower girls drop her basket. Something was wrong. Another child squealed and ran. The music broke off abruptly as the guards surged forward.

"What is it?" hissed Rosetta.

"I was afraid of this," said Laurel. "Come on, Sylvie." She took her friend's hand and hurried to the front. A woman screamed.

Reaching the podium, the first thing Sylvie noticed was the look of terror in the priest's eyes. Lord Warburton was backing away.

She glanced at Godric's back, wondering at a rip along the shoulder of his doublet and at the size of his arms. Suddenly, with a strangled cry, he whirled around, no longer Godric but the hideous Keeper of the Cave, one eye bulging and the wound on his forehead bright red. With a sweep of a powerful arm, he knocked the documents and several goblets off the table.

Screams flew from the crowd. Most of the courtiers had never seen this creature, confined as he was to the recesses of Humped Mountain. But now he stood before them, a snarling nightmare. They fell over one another trying to get away.

Sylvie knew what she had to do. It was what she did every time a Reader came to the end of the story: She had to break the spell.

"No!" Rosetta cried out. "Stop, Sylvie!"

Princess Sylvie turned in surprise.

"Thanks," said Rosetta, "but this is my job now." She stepped boldly before the Keeper of the Cave, reached an arm around his thick neck, and kissed him on his wounded forehead.

Abruptly, the creature stumbled backward, his balance off, and fell in the grass.

"Oh!" he gasped. His eyes looked wild as he attempted to rise on his elbow.

The wedding guests watched, fascinated, as his swollen brow receded, his eyes gradually became clear, and his body grew slim and youthful. He was Godric again, the golden-haired prince.

"Rose," he stammered.

She smiled down at him.

Thomas, looking shaken, helped his friend to his feet. "I thought only Princess Sylvie could do that," he murmured.

Rosetta pursed her lips into a "Shh. Don't let the Readers know."

King Walther approached. "Godric, are you all right?"

The prince still looked dazed. "I think so," he said, and felt his cheeks and forehead to be sure he was himself.

"Well then!" said the king. "Let the ceremony continue!"

The priest, his beard trembling slightly, raised his arms to begin his Lesser Old Middle High marriage chant while the waters of the Mere lapped gently in the background.

"*Sôse bênrenkî, sôse bluotrenkî, sôse lidirenkî . . .*"

"What's he saying?" Sylvie hissed under her breath.

Laurel gave a small smile. "I'm a little rusty on this. Something about bones and blood and limbs."

Suddenly there was another disruption, as upsetting as

the first. Just before the exchanging of the rings an orange-plumaged bird flew low overhead, screaming, "*Rawwwwk!* Reader!"

Sylvie looked up in dismay. "Not now!"

The bullfrogs in the Mere confirmed the news, belching, "Oooopen! Booook open!"

"But we can't!" cried Rosetta.

"We haven't a choice," King Walther called out. "Everyone to your places!"

Before anyone had a chance to move, the sunny afternoon sky lifted away, revealing a glimmering midnight above it—not the midnight of the book, with its moon and three little clouds, but the vast starry firmament of the universe. Whoever this Reader was, he was reading outside at night!

Equally remarkable, the Reader seemed interested in the same page that Rosetta's wedding was on. It was the first description of Humped Mountain, the very paragraph that the astronaut Kara had read years ago, on a frozen moon of Jupiter, when she and Wink were burying the time capsule.

A face appeared above the page. A minister of some kind, from what Sylvie could judge from his robe. His forehead was lined with years of being serious. "And now," he intoned, "before we come to the exchanging of the rings and our final blessing, Kara and Matthew have asked me to read a short passage from their favorite book."

"What?" exclaimed Sylvie.

"What did he say?" Lord Warburton craned his neck.

"Something about the astronauts?" King Walther said.

"They must have made it back!" cried Rosetta.

"It's not a long book," the minister continued, "but they tell me it saved their lives. Saved the mission itself. It's called, um, *The Very Good Thing*."

Sylvie jumped up and down. "It's called *The Great Good Thing*, you oaf!"

"Sylvie!" cautioned Queen Emmeline.

The minister started reading the passage Kara had read that deadly day in the far reaches of space. He concluded: "'She didn't know what the secret was, but she would not rest till she had discovered it, for it was the key to everything. There would be no peace in the kingdom, she knew, unless she could break the spell and make the mountain speak. The wind blew her hair across her face as the last sunlight scooped shadows in the valley. Yes, she would unlock that mountain. It was her destiny, the great good thing she was here to do.'"

The minister smiled and tilted the book down, revealing to Sylvie a multitude of people, and in the back, roped off from the crowd, a battery of television cameras. It took a moment for Sylvie to recognize the elegant couple, in bridal gown and tuxedo, standing at the front.

"They're getting married too!" Rosetta exclaimed delightedly.

"I've never been to a double wedding before," said Laurel.

"Kara and Matt and their unfortunate companion Jeff

Winkermann set forth across the depths of space," the minister was saying, his voice rising dramatically, "as the representatives of humanity, to 'unlock the mountain,' you might say, and accomplish a very good thing. . . ."

"*Great* good thing!" Sylvie shouted upward.

"And they have *done* that very good thing and have come back after eight unimaginable years to tell us what they have seen. In the process they experienced one of mankind's great miracles, the miracle of love. That miracle is what we, here outside this great observatory and people all around the world who are watching tonight's ceremony on television, are celebrating."

Rosetta turned to Laurel. "People around the world?"

"I have a feeling," Laurel answered, "that our book is going to be popular again."

"And so," the minister went on, his voice as smooth as pulled taffy, "if we are ready . . ." He cleared his throat. "Rings, please."

Laurel nudged Rosetta. "How about you? What are you waiting for?"

"What? Oh!" Rosetta whispered to the priest, who nodded and took her left hand and Godric's right in his own and resumed his chanting:

"*Bên zi bêna, bluot zi bluoda . . .*"

"Bone to bone, blood to blood," Laurel murmured under her breath.

Rosetta, although she understood very little, felt tears well up in her eyes as she gazed at her beautiful prince. Soon his eyes were glittering as well.

"Do you, Matthew David, take this woman, Kara

Elizabeth, to be your lawful wedded wife?" The minister looked from one to the other.

"I do," Matt said quietly.

"And do you, Kara Elizabeth, take this man . . ."

"Lid zi geliden . . ."

"Limb to limb," whispered Laurel.

Sylvie raised her eyes from Rose and Godric to Kara and Matt, then looked above the heads of the astronauts to the stars they'd returned from.

"I now pronounce you . . ."

"Sôse gelimida sîn!"

"What's that mean?" whispered Sylvie.

"So let them all be healed," Laurel replied.

Then the minister's voice said, "You may now kiss the bride."

Overhead, Kara and Matt kissed tenderly just as, in the pages of *The Great Good Thing*, Rosetta kissed Godric.

"Isn't that . . . ?" Sylvie murmured.

Laurel followed Sylvie's eyes. The vast night sky looked brilliant. "What?" she said.

"A little to the left."

Laurel searched the heavens. "I see it," she whispered.

"The flying woman!" Sylvie murmured.

"Yes! The constellation of Sylvie."